CW01497427

First published in Great Britain in 2025 by
Peirene Press Ltd
The Studio, 10 Palace Yard Mews
Bath BA1 2NH
www.peirenepress.com

This edition published by arrangement with Agence Catherine Nabokov
and Linwood Messina Literary Agency.

This translation © Madeleine Rogers, 2025

ISBN 978-1-908670-91-5

The authorised representative in the EU for product safety and
compliance is Easy Access System Europe, Mustamäe tee 50, 10621
Tallinn, Estonia | gpsr.requests@easproject.com

Designed by Orlando Lloyd
Printed and bound in the United Kingdom by CPI Books Ltd

The translation of this work was supported
by a grant from the CNL (Centre national
du livre) | This book is supported by the
Institut français (Royaume-Uni) as part of
the Burgess Programme.

FRIENDS AND LOVERS

Nolwenn Le Blevennec

Translated from the French
by Madeleine Rogers

PEIRENE

To Sterren.

I
SOUTH

May 23rd is not the twenty-third day of the month of May – it's Rim's birthday. That date, learned at the very start of my life, belongs to my childhood friend. It is entwined with her like a word with its object, has no existence of its own, self-destructs in the air without her. From the moment I wake up that morning, my mind is fully occupied; I think of nothing but her. Above all: don't forget to call Rim. *What do you want for your birthday? Where are you? How are you?* While Daniel makes me scrambled eggs, I revisit her family's apartment in my mind. I see us as children, curled up on her parents' adjustable electric bed. We can't stop giggling at the bit in *Dirty Dancing* when Baby says to Johnny: 'Most of all, I'm scared of walking out of this room and never feeling the rest of my whole life the way I feel when I'm with you!' I want to play the scene for a fourth time. Rim's had enough but says, 'All right, go on then'. She presses the crackling rewind button on the VCR while I use the control on her parents' bed to lay it flat. We fall about laughing again.

It's 6.30 a.m. on 23 May 2021. My adult bed doesn't move. It's a block of cement I won't leave for the day because, like I always do on 23 May, I'm setting off into the landscape of a lost friendship.

1

Champomy Gold

I've known Rim forever, but it was when she was hired by the same magazine as me, in 2010, that she took up her full place in my life again and our trio with Anna was formed. The three of us were leading similar lives, by which I mean we were at the start of our thirties and on the verge of having babies with decent guys. And by decent, I mean men who take care of at least half the domestic duties.

When she wasn't reading psychoanalysis, Anna shared her life with an Argentine documentary director whose particular talent was knowing the right thing to say to bring everyone together. His rhetorical strength: respecting everybody to the detriment of nobody. Watching Panchi's films, my mind would go blank in approval. It's intersectional respect, I would think every time, and also that he would wind up as the mayor of a little French village. Tall and thin, Panchi wore silk scarves and chunky beanies knitted by his mother. He would inhale yogurts directly from the pot while smiling from behind his dark eyelashes. He gave the kind of birthday presents that proved no conversation went unnoted. With his keen intelligence and strong sense of justice, he would make a good partner during the apocalypse. His warm caramel skin contrasted with that of Anna, who was born in Savoy. Back then, they would stay up all night discussing feminism, which seemed a bit much to me.

Rim, by contrast, refused to intellectualise anything. She lived with a blonde boy who liked to wear overly tight clothes and checked shirts open to the navel. Good-looking and vegan, with the once-a-year exception of pan-fried calamari with chickpeas and lemon. As active as Rim, Niels (the 's' is silent) was a holistic personal trainer and climbing instructor. Three mornings in the Buttes-Chaumont park spent supporting Rim's thighs, as she couldn't climb well to begin with, were enough for him to start seeing her yellow leggings everywhere around Paris, like she was stalking him. The Franco-Norwegian, awkward in conversation, was sweet in the sense that he liked to hang flowers from the ceiling. In the sense that he never smoked a cigarette without offering one to anyone around him, which is a great quality to have. When they met, Rim swapped her 'Kommandant' attitude for the total opposite – overnight she became a prancing Christmas elf.

As for me (Armelle: cinema rat; round tortoiseshell glasses; afraid of everything, all people and situations), I lived with Daniel (professor of history; ten years older than me; quick-witted; two children with another woman; a big, solid guy – you could line up marbles in the main fold of his neck when he was asleep – with a Ukrainian surname and curly black hair). Like Panchi, Daniel is politically unassailable: the emperor of the lecture hall, he's always two progressive steps ahead. A confident man when it comes to current affairs, his Twitter addiction has made him a master of the one-liner. Although I've never told him so, there are many things I love about him. How he won't start our little Colette electric car, out of respect for her, until I've shouted 'Colette turbo, turbo let's go!' How in bed, before we have sex, he speaks to me in Yiddish with a Spanish accent. How when he wakes up, he clings to me like a full moon that's been alone for too long. How his scent lingers on the sheets like a light dusting of flour. How at night his warm head sinks into the bolster (that pillow will be my top source of DNA for his reincarnation). But also how he calls me at all hours of the day to sing a duet of 'California Dreamin'' by the Mamas & the Papas. My phone rings and and he starts singing the first line in an almost unbearable range, far too shrill for a man. Silence my end. He repeats the line since I haven't launched into the second, female part, a hundred times too high for me. I'm in a meeting. I excuse myself to tell him to stop – 'Please stop, I'm at work, I can't right now' – but I always give in. He carries on, and I'm fully on board by now.

'Have a good day.'

'You too, honey.'

With these three functioning men, Rim, Anna and I had gone around exhibitions, nestled up together to read novels, organised and been subject to surprise birthday parties. Then, naturally, had babies. Because my partner was older than me, I'd got started earlier than Rim and Anna, and my second son, with hair like a motorbike helmet, was the same age as their first daughters. At the end of the summer of 2012, when we were all at different points along the Atlantic coast (La Trinité, Île d'Oléron, Saint-Pée-sur-Nivelle), we learned that all three of us were pregnant, and the WhatsApp group 'Atlantic Babies' was created. Topics covered in that group after our respective deliveries: the benefits of epidurals, anaesthetists' physiques, haemorrhoids, disposable maternity knickers, milk-swollen breasts, breasts full stop, and the use of the third-person singular by midwives and nurses ('Mummy's going to move you').

Every day, Rim expressed to the group her desire to start exercising again. But before that could happen, a depression was due. One that was difficult and unaddressed, as they say in psychoanalysis, which here means that she kept saying 'I'm fine' while she went through life holding her breath. Her clothes were black and crumpled. Her baby's crying sounded like a rebuke. She changed her on autopilot, without making eye contact. She feigned happiness in front of the neighbours. Towards the end of her maternity leave, she was sending me apartment listings on every possible channel (text, Facebook, Instagram). To the point of getting her bank account frozen, Rim was visiting apartments. To buy them. Each viewing ended with her putting in an offer at the asking price. 'Aloïs will be happy in this bedroom,' she'd say to the estate agents. 'That's my daughter, she was just born.' Seven offers and seven retractions later, I was asked to 'show up' once more in

Saint-Ouen, at 12.15 p.m. on a Tuesday: 'A follow-up visit. The last one, I promise.'

Her real-estate madness ended that day when, outside Garibaldi Métro station, I told her I wasn't going anywhere with her and that I was going to call her mother if she carried on. After that, she got back on her feet, and her tenderness for her daughter was unstoppered when, one evening when she went to pick her up from nursery, she watched her through the window for a long time and saw how nicely she played with the other children. In 2013 and 2014, Anna, Rim and I went hand in hand through the early maternity phase: the time when women are more preoccupied with their child than with any other human activity, more even than with yoga classes when trying to become a yoga instructor yourself. This period when work feels like a holiday, when a solo train journey elicits shivers of freedom, starting at the shop at the station ('I'm going to buy myself *Paris Match* and some pencils, yeah!'). But also when, once you're through the front door, you're back under the child's dictatorship, because they know how to get the best for themselves. One hand on their tummy and a nursery rhyme that makes absolutely no sense, like 'Pop goes the weasel'.

In the months following birth, a child is like an unpredictable fire alarm: the wailing is set off when there's no fire, no smoke, not so much as a match. And the new mother always seems like she's just spent three hours using her own body to clean the house. Dry hair, milk-stained clothes, she moves the play mat around for no reason. In addition – and this is as touching as it is concerning – her social identity dissolves. She babbles, spellbound, films baby's first puree, takes thousands of identical photos, worries about a collar being too tight around a neck ('Can he breathe properly, do you think? Are you sure?'). Her grey matter is pressed through a funnel that concentrates it to the extreme on issues of motherhood. She sets herself philosophical questions: *Should I put shoes on him before he can walk? And if so, why?* And practical problems: *Is his bottle flowing properly?* The answer to this type of interrogation is always no. In the middle of the night, she can be found in the kitchen, hands trembling with tiredness, opening the teat with a carving knife so the milk comes out faster, but now it'll come out too fast.

When Rim finally started exercising again, she sent me a video. A gravel path and red trainers going in and out of the frame, the sound of her heavy breathing and squeaks of joy. 'I'm running, Armelle, I'm running!' Even though I was happy to see her come back to us, I couldn't raise a smile. I'd just been shaken to my core.

Let me explain. Seconds before Rim's video arrived, I'd been added to a new WhatsApp group. Created by Daniel, it was named 'Big birthday bash this Saturday!', with nineteen unrecognised numbers. My hypothesis: for my son Gus's third birthday, shortly after I'd given birth to our second son, my partner was about to invite two-thirds of his nursery class to our place without having consulted me. 'Bash' was surely what was about to happen to me and my home. Nineteen pairs of energetic legs, running free. Thirty-eight longship oars gone crazy in my living room. For a few seconds the chat was empty. Then:

Ciao tutti! Paolo, Oscar (aka Kiki), César, Youssouf, Lila, Paul, Sacha, Milynda, Meriem, Louise, Titien, Lou, Marceau, Gabriel, Gauthier, Jeanne, Baptiste [so many other names] *are all invited Saturday lunchtime. I'll make a big platter of nuggets and chips. And of course: anyone who wants to stay over is welcome to.*

Of course.

Overjoyed at this glimpse of freedom, afraid the offer would evaporate, the other parents replied in a flurry. *Paul will be there. Cool, bringing his pyjamas? Oscar can't wait.* Fifty notifications later, I was still dumbstruck. How had Daniel got all those numbers? Was this the product of some long undercover operation, or had he got in touch with the intimidating nursery headmistress? I switched my phone to flight mode, put it down on my desk and crashed back into my leather chair. I had three and a half days ahead of me, i.e. nothing. The lifespan of a midge that had died tragically young. I googled a rule that had sprung to mind about the acceptable number of guests relative to age: one for the first birthday, two for the second, three for the third. Where had that come from? Had I invented it myself or had it been dictated by a child psychologist, an authority on the subject that I could use in opposition to Daniel? *Go on Dr Bretzel's website and you'll see how you're cocking this up.* I couldn't find anything online. That evening I was silently raging, but the sight of the father of my children in the bath, with his belly sticking out of the water like a volcano and his body pressed against the sides of the tub, softened my anger.

Then it arrived. I mean, the day of the birthday party arrived. In the blink of an eye, a crowd of large babies were in my hallway, staring at me like a glowing screen. At my feet, a growing mountain of miniature coats. Pairs of shoes violently separated and flung to all four corners of the room. Between rings of the doorbell, I went to my room to reconfigure my welcoming, motherly smile. I found the entirety of Louise in my wardrobe. 'No, those are my shoes. And I don't mean to boss you around, Louise, but I would like you to leave my bedroom. It's mine, you understand? *Mine*.' By 1 p.m., my son wasn't expecting anyone else. When the doorbell rang, I hoped it was some parents back again already, parents unused to such freedom, not knowing what to do without baby wipes and nap time, perhaps having left the cinema halfway through the film, frightened by their own relaxation and by the realm of possibilities. But that couldn't be it. As I crossed the living room to go and answer the bell, I gave Daniel an uncharacteristically nasty look. The party was in full swing. I counted the number of nuggets on the floor. I didn't count the number of smushed chips; I'd have wanted to send five street sweepers' carts through the room if I had. To be Mickey Mouse in *Fantasia* on the condition of being able to turn back into myself. I opened the door, and Rim and Anna smiled at me. 'We haven't brought our girls, I hope you're not too disappointed,' said Rim, putting her hand on my shoulder. I shook my head and murmured, 'Oh my God, thank you for coming.'

In the hallway, Rim put her big Adidas bag on the floor. She unzipped it and pulled out a clear plastic case full of face paints. Without saying a word, she carried on through the apartment and, in the middle of the living room, after a deep inhalation, yelled frighteningly loudly, 'Everyone line up. I'm gonna paint the boys as butterflies and the girls as lions!' At the same time, Anna put her arm round my neck and led me into the kitchen. From a shopping bag, she took out chocolate, butter, sugar, flour and eggs, then produced a little bag of crushed nuts from her coat pocket. She asked if I had a baking tin, then she said: 'Remind me how many children there are here.'

'I'd rather not think about it, but nineteen.'

'Amazing. That's how long we'll bake the cake for.'

'Nineteen minutes? So it melts in the middle?'

'Yeah.'

'Sorry but I'd really rather not, Anna. For the sake of my mental health. And the sofa. For their sake, even.'

'We can go for twenty-two minutes then, but it won't be as good.'

'They're only little. They won't remember.'

After the candles and the presents, Daniel offered to take the kids down to the park for a football match. It's his magic power, having ideas like that (and his magic power squared to be able to transport so many sugar-addled children without losing a single one). He makes up stories – he's got a good one about the littlest knight – and, enchanted, the children follow him closely. He put our baby in the pram, Gus's tiny guests lined up behind him, and the door closed behind the convoy. Anna, Rim and I went to sit on the round balcony outside my bedroom that I don't take enough care of (no plants, just cigarette ends; I hate myself every time I see it). Sitting on the floor, our faces turned towards the sun, we polished off two bottles of Champomy Gold, drinking the sparkling peach and apple juice straight from the bottle. Rim showed us how she pretends to be asleep at the start of the 6–8 p.m. parental tunnel, when she doesn't want to take care of anything. Mouth open, tongue hanging out the side. 'The key, really, is to look as pathetic as you can.' The role of a lifetime. Standing over her, Niels, incredulous, will say out loud: 'Fucking hell, she's taking the piss. Come on then, kids, bath time.' In the first long silence, I told them that what they'd done for me that afternoon, well, I wouldn't have done it, it would have been too much for me, but I'd be there for them in other ways. To look after their daughters overnight, for example. Because I liked the night-times. Saying *Everything's all right, it's still bedtime, here's your dummy, here you go*, and stroking their heads. Baby hair: an incredible substance that capitalism has yet to exploit. Rim replied: 'Okay, Saturday night then.' She was doing better, but her eyes still seemed wider from their fight against fatigue. She was cleaning her face paint brushes one by one in a glass of water held between her thighs and putting them back in the case. A song floated up from the apartment downstairs: '*There's a hero, / If you look inside your heart...*'

Mariah Carey. Children of the early eighties, Rim and I had sung that tune a hundred thousand times while miming a microphone with our fists. We knew the words by heart (not Anna, though – in Cluses they were cooler or less cheesy; they listened to Tryo instead). But that day, Rim and I acted like it was some foreign air, unknown in these latitudes. A strange, silent agreement. As if singing that song carried the risk of seeing materialise, before our eyes, a huge mountain of clay symbolising the time gone by since our teenage years.

'It went well, this birthday party,' said Rim.

'Yeah, really well,' I said.

2

The Great Awakening

In the same way that we'd gone through the motions of early motherhood in a daze, as though we'd been wandering, drunk and barefoot, through the early-morning streets, feeling both unaware of ourselves yet full of joy and love, we didn't notice this time coming to an end. But if I think about it, the turning point came on a Sunday in October 2014. That day, in Anna's living room, which looked down onto the forecourt of the Gare de Lyon, Adèle stood up. The little girl who smelled of figs took her first steps, with the aim of grabbing her mother's iPhone and throwing it on the floor. And I like to think that when the phone hit the ground, an energy was set loose and at the other end of Paris, at Rim's apartment in Montmartre and, more precisely, in her head, the idea of a trip was formed. To reinvigorate us, leave this inertia behind and close off this critical phase of our lives. To mark the fact that there had been a passage, a profound change; that we were on the other side now, the side of adults, of parents, but that everything was going to be fine, it wasn't like it was a prison. Lying on her sofa, a sliver of her

22

breast lit up by the sun, her daughter asleep on her stomach, Rim thought of Tunisia. Partly because she loves harissa so much she's always put it in her spaghetti. She held on to the idea all day, and then all night too, which was more difficult. The next morning, she was still thinking about it when we arrived at the office at the same time and walked across the last zebra crossing like the Beatles. Once through the revolving door, we greeted Robert, who was eating mini pastries and watching MMA videos. 'Go, go, go, two minutes!' he cried, holding the mail out to Anna. In front of the lift, Rim let out a longer yawn than usual, the back of her hand against her mouth. I imitated her, and in that sleep-deprived gesture she must have seen the confirmation that her idea was a good one. She seemed to be waiting for the noise of the lift, which was still floors away. Our knees, all in a row, were wet with the tepid October rain. Well then? She made a quarter-turn towards us, our faces still in profile, and said: 'Come on, we've suffered enough. We have the right to a bit of freedom. Let's do something for ourselves. Let's go and spend Christmas in Midoun.'

Midoun? The town sounds like the surname of a foreign grandmother handing out honey (mine, the one I knew best, made me eat horse, which is pretty much the opposite). So on hearing that word – and I don't know how else to explain it – my skull filled with a celestial light. My neural pathways were bathed in white fog. Something had become possible because our motherly arms were suddenly empty. Our children having simultaneously assumed vertical positions, becoming bipeds of the same order as the ostrich, what was to be done with the great void left on our torsos and our hips? A phenomenon of psychological and bodily reappropriation followed, logical but unconscious. The return of wishful thinking. All three of us were on the brink of what I now call the Great Awakening. And it would start with a flash of lucidity about our post-maternity futures. After so many biological processes and all the logistical nightmares involving the folding cot, after so much emotion and adaptation, the mind realises it's trapped in a never-ending familial motif. The future takes the form of a long, narrow, uniform corridor. Wallpapered with a Machiavellian design. A single geometric pattern as far as the eye can see. Fleurs-de-lys, for example. Small. Yellow. Terribly symmetrical. Repeated along the entire length of existence. Into infinity. Which is to say, if we drop the metaphor: the same family forever. The same noses, the same pores, the same personality flaws. Basically, the same individuals – whom we love, of course, more than words can say, but who eat us alive and for whose benefit, too, a consumerist mania swings into action. Shampoo, shoes, dinosaur figurines, ham, swimming costumes. The family: a genetic product trapped in an economic unit. So, no more surprises. Organs that no longer surge with emotion but simply fill up and empty out. Parks, Monopoly and death. There's your itinerary.

And then? Then, no. Shortly after, what happens in some women – thankfully not all of them – is that the desire to fight back is born. That's the great awakening. A somersault. Or, if you prefer, a blazing post-maternity rebellion. Emma Bovary is its patron saint, not just for her infatuations and flirtatiousness in themselves but also for her intrepid spirit of decision. Because the idea or urge isn't to disrupt this neatly mapped-out future for the purpose of regaining career ambitions or discipline, which would be honourable, laudable and socially useful (if this regained energy were invested in geoengineering, for example), but to plunge your head, your whole head, back into the waters of love. To exhaust your sexual potential the way you might fritter an inheritance before killing yourself. And to that end, the game of cards begun ten years earlier with the lovely father of your children is set aside. *Put yourself down here for a second.* At the precise moment of awakening you listen to your gut as if at a door; the urge is to go elsewhere and start all over again. Cruelly. *I don't want you in that way any more, that's it.* All that to feel something again, rather than for the reality of someone else. Indeed, at this stage of life, taking a lover has more purpose than ever. It's compensation for the constraints of motherhood. For the years when your body was accommodation. The night-time bookkeeping: *It's your turn to go.* The scoliosis lunchtimes: the pieces of bread picked up once, twice, three times, etc. The every-other-Saturday sex and the ridiculous arguments (there were four half-full Volvic bottles on his side of the bed so I added two more to wind him up). After all that, you need a second wind. And to forget for a brief while that our youth disappears as quickly as water poured on sand. A woman's days are numbered. So these unsettled new mothers get restless. They stage terrible, brilliant scenes all around them. Love and violence, sorrow, physical tension. Why shouldn't a despairing lover self-immolate beneath their window? Everything they do is to feel more alive, more radiant, more intensely themselves. Like a musical toy that won't switch off, blasting its tune until its batteries run out.

And maybe, thinking about it, this sexual *Great Awakening* also takes place to quieten the fear of death that strikes when your children are small. I say this because at the time I thought a lot about the psychological impact my own death would have on my boys. I thought, very humbly, of how it would stop them in their tracks and perhaps make great painters of them, or total wrecks (or both). In *Darkness Visible*, William Styron writes that he is convinced his alcoholism has its roots in his mother's death when he was thirteen, which isn't that young. I don't say this to absolve us, but I think that this – this pathetic rebellion, this thrashing around of the near-forty-year-old caught in a trap, this rapacity of new mothers that has so far escaped study by the social sciences and that bonded us, Rim, Anna and me, after our children were born, even more strongly than motherhood itself, and pushed us towards Tunisia – is widespread. You could even say that, under certain hormonal conditions, it's a case of women's bodies acting of their own accord. Knowing themselves to still be fertile, they leave in total autonomy in search of other gene pools. If that turns out to be true, has this been happening to us since prehistoric times? In any case, we went through it, this mutiny, like three sisters.

If the word 'Midoun' had such an effect on me, it's because I was depressed. In addition to my work at the magazine and the lack of solitude due to my overlarge family, those were rainy days and, at thirty-four, I'd just had my first gastroscopy-colonoscopy. Twenty-four hours before Anna's phone crashed to the floor, I was lying on my left side on the edge of an operating table. My get-up: a surgical cap, stockings and a gown made from an indeterminate material somewhere between paper and plastic. A short gown, so not a good day for my pale and spotty legs. In the distance, I could see unconscious bodies going by on wheeled stretchers. Perhaps the doctors push the critical cases up to the overground Métro line and throw them over the edge, I was thinking. Lying on the table, the irreversibility of the moment was getting to me. Anaesthesia produces a terrible pre-guillotine feeling. I was going to be put under then penetrated by camera tubes inserted through the mouth and anus. Shortly before I was hooked up to the drip, I'd imagined the two probes greeting each other in the centre of my body with the light displays probes typically make, which made me smile. As I felt myself go, I asked myself more seriously what the difference was between me and a goat keeled over dead on its side.

Two hours later, everything had gone well, but in the post-operative haze the animal confusion in my head continued; as I gnawed on the brioche from my meal tray, I felt like an old, bulimic hamster. The doctor was a bit embarrassed as he asked me to stop my crazed gobbling so he could tell me about the anomaly they'd detected in my stomach. As it turned out, there were small-intestine cells in there. Hiding out in my stomach. I was shocked. I knew you could substitute one thing for another. One person for another, yes, that too I could understand. But one part of the body where another should be? I didn't know that was possible, and it felt serious. So Midoun – 'on Djerba', Rim clarified as she got into the lift at the office – was a matter of survival. 'Okay,' I said, falling into step behind her. Holding her finger down on the button for our floor, which had lit up pale yellow, Anna added: 'I'm in too. If we can offset the carbon footprint and you let me sort out the hotel.' We nodded and, later on, when Rim and I were no longer thinking about it, Anna emailed us photos of the royal suite of a hotel called Azur Palace. A beautiful apartment in sunset tones. Thinking she'd sent it for a laugh, I replied *PERFECT* and Rim something similar, also in all caps. Five minutes later, and despite the fact that the real yes, the one that's decided at home after you've tested the impact of the no on your conscience, hadn't yet been voiced, Anna dropped the suite reservation in an attachment. Her email consisted of no words, only an image of the Tunisian desert and a link to the hotel website, which I clicked on. From a bird's-eye view, a U-shaped building lay on the sand, like a lover trying to pull the sea towards him. The description: *On the edge of the Gulf of Gabes, in the south-east of Tunisia, the Djerba 5* Azur Palace is located on the biggest island in North Africa: Djerba. Just a few steps from the most beautiful beaches on the island and less than ten minutes from the town centre, we're perfectly located for your convenience.*

Rim and I shot each other a worried look across the office. How much was this whole affair going to cost us? In response, I called for the three of us to have lunch at the Indian restaurant on the corner. A big plate of masala rice was placed in the middle of the table. Seeing my expression, Anna, unaware of her own love–hate relationship with luxury, justified herself: 'I like hotels that feel like entire towns. And you know I love concrete. If it's too expensive, I'll pay two-thirds.'

We left on the first Saturday of the 2014 Christmas holidays. Once inside Charles de Gaulle's Terminal E, we were drunk on freedom. Rim was wearing a gold bumbag round her waist and a baggy tracksuit. We felt young again, laughing as we pulled on the same stretchy croissant. Happy to be together, linked at the elbows, we boarded our Transavia plane like triplets who'd won the lottery. Hands full with coffee, books, tote bags. No pushchairs. We smiled widely at the cabin crew, who smiled right back. During take-off and the first decisive turns, I accompanied the aeroplane mentally to lend it strength. Then, as the motorways of the Val-d'Oise came to life below us, I drifted off while watching Rim take photos of clouds shaped like sheep. Two hours later, the poetry having entirely worn off, she shook me as if I were a farmer sleeping on the job. I cried out in surprise. She gave me a hard look. My head had slumped down on my tray table, and 'past a certain age, Armelle, sedatives or no, everyone knows you have to put it away for landing'.

Until that day, I had only guessed at the reasons behind this rule. As a flight attendant was going past anyway, and I was still hazy and disinhibited from the medication, I demanded an explanation. Here's the only information I managed to retain from that journey: the rule is not in place, as I had thought, to stop us crushing our bodies in the event of being thrown forwards, but to reduce the time taken to evacuate the aircraft in the event of an accident. These words made my blood boil. 'How many crashes have you heard of that turned out okay because the tray tables were up?' I asked Rim. Then, freewheeling, i.e. answering myself: 'None, of course, it's just like the inflatable boats in case of a water landing – a big myth.' Historically irritated by my fear of flying, which I've recently been masking behind environmental convictions, Rim put her headphones back on.

In Djerba, we were dazzled by the light of the south. The airport was comprised of a single runway, a single terminal. Walking over the tarmac, I concentrated on the visual clues confirming that we'd arrived in Tunisia and not some other country. Halfway down the queue for customs, we took our jumpers off. Just before we got to the counter, Anna pulled our three entry documents from her pocket, already filled out in biro, which made me realise that that had never happened to me before – filling in these forms with the right kind of pen. I could have kissed her. Once we'd collected our bags, we each withdrew the same amount of money, a thousand Tunisian dinars, before getting into a taxi with mummified seat belts. Putting mine on proved impossible, so I whispered in Rim's ear, a little too close, that I was afraid we'd have an accident, and she looked at me as if to say *Hey, you're really a parody of yourself when it comes to travelling, you know?* And also *You should be thanking me: I've been putting up with your phobias for nearly thirty years now.*

3

The Statue on Boulevard d'Inkermann

My childhood friend looks like a petite, muscular rock star. The gap between her front teeth doesn't bother her any more; neither does the scar like a stalk cutting through her upper lip. Her catlike eyes are the grey colour of the TGV trains, which could be beautiful. She has good bone structure, a pointy and pierced right ear, very black hair, a flat stomach and wide ribs. Let's say she's the love child of Amy Winehouse and Béatrice Dalle. Socially, she plays the part of the carefree, light-hearted girl, though really she has dark, artistic undercurrents. At work, similarly, she spends her time camouflaging her talents. She quickly taps out her music columns on the Google Docs app on her phone; she's always thought of her employers as parrots you just need to throw a few seeds to. It's from her that I got this little saying: 'One phone meeting and the whole day is fucked.' The question that torments me, and apparently only me, on Sunday evenings never even occurs to her: *If someone were to go through the archives of our magazine in a hundred and twenty years, what would they think?* What she enjoys most is hanging out behind her Yamaha keyboard, composing music in her funny little apartment. In the years before Djerba, a financial chasm had opened between us. Her salary was eaten up by concert tickets, whereas I spent my evenings watching old films at home. This thorny game of Monopoly can threaten friendships. But ours continued. I've slept with her feet in my face hundreds of times and first discovered what male genitalia look like from her father's tendency to wander naked around their family home.

I met Rim in the private gardens of a modern apartment block in Neuilly-sur-Seine, a wealthy suburb of west Paris. We were five years old. The building was on Boulevard d'Inkermann, a long artery lined with chestnut trees and perpendicular to another road, Boulevard Bineau, which drains vehicles of every shape and size crossing the Île de la Jatte at high speed to get from Colombes to Paris. Its geometric foyer was lined with bay windows and decorated with cement trays of pebbles. I had always wanted to slide along the grey-whorled marble floor in my socks, but the doorman's unmatched hatred of children stopped me. From my third-floor balcony, its floor sooty and black with dust, a sort of open-air storeroom surrounded by more elegant replicas filled with flowers, I would listen to the joyful pigeons and admire my treasure, a bag of decomposing conkers. On Sunday mornings, if I got up early enough, I would see Nicolas Sarkozy, then the mayor of Neuilly, out jogging surrounded by his bodyguards. On the pavement across the road, he once stopped exactly opposite me. He drenched himself in water, shaking his head like he was in a shower gel advert. I imitated the cry of a baby eagle, with theatrical intent. He turned his head towards me. I pretended to move the chairs around on my balcony. The implicit message was: no one cares that you run here.

One autumn evening in 1985, I was playing on the stone ledges in the garden, already suffering from intrusive thoughts implying my death or the death of my loved ones: *If you fall off the wall, Mummy will die tomorrow.* Since the mobile phone hadn't been invented yet, my mother was staring into space when a woman and her daughter, both blessed with black hair and grey eyes, came crunching down the leaf-strewn pathway. Rim's mother was wearing a short evening dress in midnight blue. Her calves smelled freshly waxed. Her face belonged to the bird family, I thought, because that was my little game at the time. Looking between my mother and me, she said, 'Hello, hello.' Then, pointing out a ground-floor apartment on the left behind a hedge, she told us that the family had just moved here from the Place de la République the week before. Rim was having trouble getting used to the three-month-old baby brother whom she was holding responsible for this move, she added to try to make us laugh. I was five years old, I didn't know the Place de la République, I'd certainly never been there, but I was sure this word 'move' wasn't nearly strong enough and didn't come close to describing this transition from the world of the living towards the void. Neuilly, with its boulevards absent to themselves. A deaf universe, wide arteries echoing with nothing. The incarnation of the adjective 'residential', in its most negative connotation. From her square, badly soundproofed bedroom, Rim had heard my little voice, decided it was her salvation and asked her mother to go and look outside. Good instinct: we have twenty-five days between us (she's older) and dysfunctional families in common. Our mothers got acquainted without overdoing it. They stood a metre apart, arms folded. I imagine them that first time, in front of the manicured shrubs, complaining about the lack of shops: 'Not even a boulangerie within a kilometre!' But, having chosen to live there, maybe they didn't.

That day, Rim and I sealed our friendship playing hopscotch on the big paving stones. During that game, huge efforts were made on both our parts to make love blossom. After that we saw more and more of each other, and from the age of seven onwards not a day of my childhood went by without seeing her. Going to call on her did require courage, however. On leaving my apartment, I had to go down a miserable corridor whose surfaces were all covered with the same rust-coloured carpet. No windows. I felt like I was shut inside a taped-up shoebox. The only openings to the outside were the peepholes of the eight numbered doors that faced each other, four on one side and four on the other, as if they were about to start a danse macabre. Ever since, I've always felt that peepholes are an abuse of power from the people on the inside towards the people on the outside. By the time I got to the lift, having passed in front of all these Cyclopes, the fear was overwhelming. I would press the button and wait, my body as still as if there had been a slug crawling over my cheek. If after three minutes it hadn't arrived, I'd resign myself to pushing open the fire door that led to the staircase, an extension of the basement, a cold, echoing column where my fear was entirely renewed. By the time the door slammed behind me, I would have already run all the way down. On the ground floor there were another two heavy doors to reach Rim's corridor, which was the same as mine but shorter. The amputated version. Her apartment was the one at the very end.

If I made this journey several times a day, it was because I loved Rim and because things weren't going well at home. My parents' relationship was in such a terrible state that there wasn't space for anything else between our walls. Our living room was decorated with glass nesting tables and exhibition catalogues. Not a single toy on the floor. No trace of me anywhere. We never watched films as a family – when I saw *La Grande Vadrouille* for the first time at the age of thirty, I came up with the Louis de Funès scale: the older you are when you come across this actor for the first time, the worse your family life has been. Dinner was rushed through in the kitchen. I always devoured mine. I held my fork like a tennis racket, but no one cared. One evening, my father was telling us something. My mother, in an attempt to liven up the conversation, reacted with shock, and exclaimed, 'Oh no, surely not?!' He took it as though she really was doubting what he was saying and left the table, knocking over his adjustable stool. 'To hell with these fucking dinners,' he said. I was mortified, but I agreed with him: *Yeah, come on, let's get it over with.* 'Strawberry or apricot yogurt?' my mother asked, holding back tears.

'Strawberry,' I replied, put out that no one was asking for a divorce straight away.

Every night, the fact that our apartment was only a two-bed forced my parents' reluctant bodies to share the same space. Their bedroom, and the night-time dramas that could take place within, unsettled me profoundly, but as the rest of the apartment unsettled me even more, I always wound up outside their door. There, at the back of the apartment, wearing several pairs of pyjamas on top of each other to make things more difficult for any would-be rapist, I examined the series of dark doorways: anyone who can tolerate the sight of such a *mise en abyme* is psychologically robust. Having crept through the rooms, I opened their door a millimetre at a time, before edging forward on my stomach as slowly and surely as a glacier melting. At the foot of my mother's side of the bed, I would fall asleep, wishing never to resemble what this relationship was doing to them. I found myself in a deep identity crisis, caught between two anti-models – the victim, lying desecrated on the ground, and the tormentor who only listens to their own voice. Two hours later, I was always noticed. When she took me back to my own bed, my mother stayed for the time it took my terror to subside, endlessly stroking her index finger along my arm. We're talking about just enough patience for the parent to feel smug. Starting at daybreak, my father filled the rooms with jazz, which hindered any kind of conversation. I would get out of bed and wiggle my toes to the rhythm of the drums. I remember thinking that my father wouldn't be able to stay on his feet without that music.

That it was his very substance, what he had instead of an inner life. That was the situation at home.

Everything was also going badly outside the house, mostly because of Jacadi. While all the other girls at school wore this brand's smock dresses and wool tights, my clothes tended to come from Fabio Lucci, a discount shop in the 19th arrondissement better known for its pots and plug adaptors. The deals were great, sure, but I lived in a rich neighbourhood where the girls spent their weekends at the Paris Country Club. Dressed like that, as if for no other reason than to protect me from the cold, I was precluded from any social bonding. Thinking about it, maybe money was what was keeping my mother afloat in a universe void of tenderness. Like the thing about putting on your own oxygen mask before helping anyone else on the plane. Or the thing of having your own breakfast before making your children's (I do that, I'll admit – coffee before anything else). The main thing was for her not to go under, so she did well. In any case, it was undoubtedly from one of those ten-franc baskets that the top and then the bottoms of my purple tracksuit were pulled. Questions in the playground: 'Did you go jogging with ABBA this morning?'

That wasn't the end of my sartorial woes. Underneath this synthetic purple ensemble – a Power Ranger lost in Neuilly-sur-Seine – my underwear was holey or torn, or both. Even now, when I wear a normal pair of knickers (so almost every day) I feel like I have magic powers. On a school trip once, when it was time to give out the laundry that didn't have name labels (all my clothes), one of the leaders waved a pair of my knickers in the air, saying, 'Whose are these?' I was sitting at the back of the group, right behind a boy I liked. Mortified, I inspected the lines on my shoes as if under a microscope. My room-mate elbowed me. 'Aren't those your pants?' I could have killed her. 'Mine? Haha. You must be joking.' She insisted: 'Yeah, they are. Look at the cherries!' How did this bitch recognise the pattern on this scrap of cloth that looked like it had been buried underground for a century? The group started to laugh. 'That's a duster, miss!' The leader held the stretched, discoloured bit of fabric, which was coming apart at the seams, by her fingertips. Soon, all you'd be able to do would be to stick it to your crotch and hope it wouldn't come out of your trouser leg. Or use it to mop orange juice off the floor. 'Look, if no one claims it, it's going in the bin and it won't be any great loss!' Okay, go on then. Because of this problem with claiming my laundry, my drawers gradually emptied, trip by trip.

There was no respite, since at the end of Year 5 my school organised a fair on the well-worn theme of the ocean. It was 4.30 p.m., but the playground was as bright as if it had been midday. The sun beat down on the heads of the parents running stalls (who are these devoted adults, what hormone do they have that I'm deficient in?). One after the other, the girls arrived dressed up as mermaids, with one among them particularly magnificent: delicate, a wide Julia Roberts smile, wavy blonde hair held back by a diamond tiara, and a fishtail in black sequins. Mermaids: the obvious choice. Other than me, the only girl who stood out from

39

the crowd was dressed as a Jacques Tati-style beachgoer (the right idea, in my opinion; she turned out well in the end, by the way). I, on the other hand, turned up dressed as a fishing net. A blue dress – shapeless, long, dragging over the floor like the tide – made of crêpe paper representing the sea, with a rigging on the front that my grandmother had attached thousands of seashells to. As I walked, they tinkled. When I ran, I made the sound of a pot of mussels being tipped onto a plate. To make matters worse, I was quite round at that point because I dipped my Camembert sandwiches in Nesquik every teatime. I was an overweight fishing net. An allegory of overfishing.

In our Year 5 photo, I'm not smiling. I have the expression of a convict and my ink-covered fingers are resting on the shoulder of a pupil who (and I know it too) has me round to her house every Wednesday afternoon against her will because our mothers made an agreement at the start of the year. In the photo, my blue hand is holding on to her yellow jumper. The girl is grimacing with bitterness. Her mouth is twisted, and that makes a little hollow of irritation inside her cheek. I've irritated people since, but never so much as then. The day the photo was given out, she lost it at me. I understood her reasons.

After these mishaps, I would go and curl up with Rim, who had the same problems as me at the local private school but who complained about it less. Her family situation was equally desperate. Her father, who worked at the Ministry of Economy, Finance and Industry, had been raised with the idea that a man's life is a success as long as he never touches a sponge. Every Thursday evening, he went to eat oysters at La Coupole with his colleagues. It was the era of ubiquitous suits and ties. Who knows where they went after dinner, but Jean-Jacques would come home with eyes as blurred and watery as the molluscs he was digesting. In the morning, the bathroom would be found in a state of devastation, as if someone had burst a piñata filled with toiletries. The toothpaste cap in the bathtub, floss in the toilet, etc. Nicknamed Jiji, Jean-Jacques looked like Claude Brasseur, and every Sunday, irritated by our childish noisiness, he made as if to take control of our upbringing. So he would tell us to sit up, that dinner was ready, that we must let the adults help themselves first, even if that meant you wound up with nothing but chicken breast on your plate (and a dry mouth for the rest of your life). Having set this straight, he would turn on the news so as not to have to talk to us about his work at the ministry, which no one understood at any rate. In the eighties, with the tertiary sector exploding, jobs were prolific, nebulous, purposeless. My own parents worked in media planning.

As for Rim's mother, she was simply odd. Among other quirks, she had changed her name when she was twenty, from Estelle to Emmanuelle, without saying anything, as if before that everyone else had been getting it wrong. She was as lanky as her daughter was compact. Her eyebrows were drawn on with red pencil. Her best quality: the precise way she drove her Autobianchi. Her worst quality: everything else. Her main problem was how she permanently conflated

Rim with herself. Her daughter wasn't a separate individual but an amputated limb, misplaced flesh, a territory under the governance of the motherland. My friend's existence interested her only insofar as it enhanced her own image. An image she enhanced herself through the tall tales she endlessly told Rim and me. For example, although the travel agency she managed was a humble one near the Neuilly town hall, next to a tanning salon, she claimed to have a number of international heads of state among her clients. In the evenings, through the half-open bathroom door, she would relate her phone calls with them, soaping herself as she divulged the number of the flight to Hawaii she'd booked the day before for Bill Clinton and his mistress (this was how I discovered how sensual a whispered alphanumerical code – 'AA423' – can be). We knew it wasn't true. The body knows. But we didn't realise yet what the ramifications of this would be. A child who understands that their parent is deluded maintains a solid grip on reality, but everything they hear after that point has to be internally verified. They become an active listener, which separates them from others. In *Mother* by Luc Lang, the narrator resists the danger of believing in his mother's daydreams. He recoils, digs his heels in, turns to stone. Rather that than risk being pulled 'into the depths of the mists of time'.

Once out of her scalding-hot bath, Emmanuelle would watch *Droopy*. Sitting there, wrapped in her towel on the living-room sofa, a packet of Prince biscuits resting on her belly, she seemed to have regressed, perhaps to an age where something had gone wrong. One time, we saw her giggling at the eight o'clock news, biting her hand to stop herself from laughing too loudly. On-screen, a boy with Down's syndrome was describing his difficulties at school. That's my memory of her that chills me the most. Much later, when I read Freud's *The Schreber Case* on Anna's recommendation, I had to stop myself from sending screenshots of certain passages to Rim, because you never know what a text message might be interrupting. A text's meaning depends entirely on the mood of its recipient. In the end I waited to see her in person to tell her that we're wrong to associate paranoia with delusions of persecution, which is actually just one of its extreme manifestations. Because the 'paranoid character' is identifiable above all by how their libido is only used to inflate their own ego. According to the psychiatrist Georges Lantéri-Laura, this pathology is characterised by pride (false modesty), suspicion (or excessive susceptibility), false judgement (on the basis of preconceived notions) and social maladjustment (aggression towards others). It's a structural defect that leads them to project their suffering and their pseudo-wrongdoings onto others. Their delusion isn't spectacular, it's a rhetorical choice. A conversational filter. Every day, their body expels hatred which is aimed at those around them, but it spares some to create contrast. Over lunch, Rim only half-listened. She's not interested in psychology.

*

On this 23 May morning, I turn on my bedside lamp. I slide a hand under the bed and find the old Dr Martens shoebox where I keep my childhood photographs. I set it down on myself. I'm searching for a particular photo. Rim, her mother and I are about to get on a ski chairlift, under a blue sky. My friend and I are posing side-on, our arms in a Z-shape: an Egyptian pose. We're eight years old. In the foreground, in a belted yellow snowsuit, sunglasses on top of her head, Emmanuelle is creasing up as if Charlie Chaplin were coming at her in the snowplough position. In reality there's nothing in front of her at all, only the valley echoing her laughter back at her.

*

Among these two family shipwrecks, the only person we could really count on was Rim's paternal aunt, whom I loved because she let us binge-watch cartoons until our eyes went square. Karine was a doctor, a narcoleptic and a Roselyne Bachelot lookalike. Her scientific education meant she was capable of working out enormous square roots in her head, but her condition led her to fall asleep any time and anywhere, even in the middle of a meal. These naps allowed us to have dinner several times over. (At that time, Rim and I were so insatiable that we'd sometimes get up in the night to eat cold leftover pasta.)

The summer we were ten, it was 9 p.m. and we were drinking chocolate milk with straws in the kitchen. All of a sudden, Rim said: 'Let's climb the statue.' I knew she was talking about the Duke of Orléans and his thoroughbred, both made of bronze, who stood guard over the end of

Boulevard d'Inkermann. Rim estimated that we'd need a chair to reach the horse's hindquarters. We stupidly opted for a Louis XVI armchair with sculpted, slippery elbow rests. Incomprehensible in hindsight. We carried it on its side, and I was silently fuming to have got the backrest (although I wouldn't have liked the feet either). Karine was asleep against the piano, right on the floor. The doorman wasn't at his post. The coast was clear. Five hundred metres of street to cover; we covered them. Thanks to the chair, and in yet another demonstration of her physical strength, Rim easily hauled herself onto the horse's rump. I got up on the armchair in turn, but I couldn't manage to pull myself up onto the saddle. Rim pulled on my arm, which permanently messed up my elbow (it still bothers me on rainy days). Eventually I got a foot onto the horse's tail, pushed hard and got up there myself too. At 9.30 p.m., there I was behind her. We were in the saddle and the evening light was imperceptibly fading. I took my shoes off for the feeling of liberty. Rim imitated the sound of a horse's hooves, clicking her tongue. Blossom was falling around her. Rim put her hands on the duke's shoulders and assured him of our determination: 'Sir, we're your daughters and we'll run away with you because it's awful here.' He accelerated. The horse's flanks were warm beneath my legs. They were spread too wide, but I tried not to think about it. Soon we would be galloping. I held Rim by the waist and squeezed her hard, which she put up with. The duke's jacket was creased. The horse set off and, just as I thought my hair was going to whip up and the horse was going to take off through the air and touch down in a land with no corridors or peepholes, an old lady cried out: 'No! What are you doing up there? Get down at once or I'll call the police. Little rascals!' Then she called out to her husband, who was walking ahead of her: 'Pierre! Pierre, would you look at these two little vandals!' Pierre glanced over his shoulder but didn't deem it worth stopping for. Standing there in her disapproval, the old lady did a little penguin dance, her arms flapping against the sides of her fur coat. Then our youth, our devastated demeanour and our hurry to get down from the horse seemed to defuse her. After a last gesture with her chin, she turned and ran after her husband. I thought: *Past a certain age, people don't let themselves climb on horse statues any more, but then what's the point of them?* When we got home, our muddy shoes dirtied the marble floor in the lobby. The armchair, which we no longer had the strength to lift, left stripy scratch marks in several places. For months afterwards, the doorman seemed to be suppressing the urge to strangle us every time we crossed paths with him. He didn't have any proof that it was us.

4

The Djellaba

In the taxi on the way to the hotel, I thought about my children, who would climb all over the street furniture if I ever let them go around Paris on their own – I haven't decided yet if I will. I imagined the cold holidays they'd be having: *What will they think, when they're old enough to think anything about it, of this week I spent in the sun over Christmas without them? Will they be cross, or congratulate me for it?* We were going too fast, and the unspoken discomfort was only increased when 'Sur la route' by Gérald de Palmas started playing on the Tunisian radio. *Why this song, as if we were in a Carrefour supermarket?* This question reached the front seat of the car, and Rim's horrified look – she's the most sensitive to incongruous audio (even though we were in fact, like in the song, on the road) – made me shake with laughter. From then on I watched her eyes as they skipped from one flamingo to the next. The birds lined the road, standing still and slender in the water, right by the edge of the carriageway. 'Sleeping or drinking... They don't have many options,' said Anna. 'Either way, they live together in harmony,' I said, making a mental note to google 'flamingo fight' ASAP.

At the Azur's imperial entrance gate, our identities were checked: first by a young boy in a fluorescent-yellow Nike cap, then an older gentleman who looked identical to him but was wearing an age-appropriate mustard-coloured shirt. Well known for its kosher buffet and kippa-wearing clientele, the hotel had particularly stringent security. In the lobby inundated with golden luggage trolleys, the ceiling was stunningly high, easily ten metres – I could see Anna was absolutely thrilled by it. Before taking us to our room, the receptionist wanted to show us around the spa, which was called the Blue Ocean Institute. A sort of palace inside a palace. She threw open the doors of each massage cabin as if she were throwing heavy ropes around a sailing ship; with each one we were obliged to come up with a new expression of enthusiasm. Then she took us to see the heated swimming pool in the shape of a pond, under a glass roof. We patiently stepped over colourful rubber rings as we followed her. I inhaled the scent of chlorine; Anna hooked her arm through mine.

'I want nothing to do with heated pools. You know the thing about the frog in the boiling water?'

'Of course. I think about it every time I take a bath.'

'You're scared you'll cook?'

'Exactly.'

'Cold water has a better reputation,' Anna said, settling her gaze on the swimming pool.

'But that's very dangerous too. Your blood leaves your

extremities and rushes to the centre of your body – boom, cardiac arrest.'

'How long do you think we'd survive in the sea in Brittany in winter?'

'With those currents? Ten minutes at most.'

*

Three years later, Rim would try, in a way, to answer Anna's question, and thinking back to that conversation now makes me feel like everything was decided as we stared into that turquoise crucible in Djerba. Everything had been going as well as it could for us (a perfectly executed choreography of work, relationships, children), until this trip to Tunisia signalled the return of the egos that had been dissolved in motherhood. The return of the Higher Self, to the detriment of the family. The sin of pride, of individualism – maybe a karmic countdown started ticking at the lacquered wood counter of the Azur's five-star spa.

This 23 May, the silence of my bedroom is making me irrational. The bedside lamp is giving me a headache. Really, I know full well that any accident depends on ten thousand factors.

*

In the heated swimming pool, several women in those ERES swimming costumes with the scalloped edges were splashing around. Among them was an ash-blonde I'd clocked because she was talking to the staff in such an ostentatiously familiar way at check-in. I'd heard her announce that her husband and children had told her at the last minute that they'd rather stay in Geneva. She could understand why: they'd been coming here for Christmas for twenty years and they were sick of it. But as she'd recently come through a serious depression and electroshock treatment, changing her routine seemed too risky. Being here brought back good memories and she had an 'awesome itinerary' lined up for the week. Massages and reading. 'I should never have given up work at thirty,' she'd added; no one replied. In the water, she was wearing pink goggles and scissoring her long legs. Further away, leggy teenagers with long hair, baseball caps and iPhones were sitting around on the deckchairs, looking unready to take on the challenge of global warming.

The lifts in this immense hotel were algorithmic (you pressed the button for the floor you wanted and waited for the lift best positioned to take you there) and the bedrooms were arranged around an empty oval space like a well, covered by a transparent dome. You couldn't see, but could tell from the noise, that this central area served as an aviary for tiny birds that spent their lives darting around three big tropical trees. Our suite on the top floor was composed of two apartments joined by a mango-wood door, each with a bedroom, a lounge and a bathroom equipped with a Jacuzzi with no instructions (I've learned that in these scenarios it's better not to bother). The floor tiles inside were as icy as the Brittany waters we'd just been discussing. The hotel's private beach with its white sand and curving palm trees stretched away from the foot of the building. Out on the balcony, Anna asked in a low voice if this stretch of coast saw migrants disembarking from Libya. And if that was the case, in what condition? No one said anything – it was the sort of thing you had to think about first. Rim remarked that the breeze was 'cooler than it looks' and that she wished she'd brought her keyboard, which no one responded to either. I was scanning the beach and remembering the attack that had taken place a year earlier, further to the north. A jihadist disguised as a tourist had pulled an AK-47 from under a parasol. Convinced that I was capable of recognising a terrorist from a distance, even those who were trying not to look like one, I now risked being constantly on the lookout. Closing the French window of the balcony behind me, I suggested we order some fruit and yogurt. Ten minutes later, a basket of peaches and three large metal domes each containing an industrial quantity of yogurt came through the door, followed by an older woman in uniform. Hot on her heels was a gold trolley full of suitcases being pushed by a young man (no cap). Anna handed them each a note with the anxious attitude of someone who doesn't know the customs. She took a Coke from the minibar and a packet of sweets from her suitcase. When the door was closed again, we got changed and each of us noticed the others' nudity in our peripheral vision.

We left our room and hurtled down the staircase that allowed access to the beach without going back through the lobby. A towel, a jumper and a book in hand, like in a Sagan novel. Rim wore her black hair in a bun, and a blood-red dress. Béatrice Dalle in *Betty Blue*. Sculpted calves and arms. An anklet. The body of a trapeze artist, you know? Anna's chest was squeezed into a sunflower-patterned bodysuit, a long skirt over the top. I was wearing a black tank top and denim dungarees, and freckles were already starting to cover my forearms; I was twelve years old again. As we walked across the sand, I thought we didn't look too bad. But I also noticed that no one else was taking any notice. We could have been peeled off the beach like an old sticker and there would have been no protests. A guy in his forties with firm buttocks, lying on his front, not bad-looking, greying under a Ricard bucket hat, was watching a pretty girl sitting at the edge of the water, her legs in the sea. The water was inoffensive, I deduced by the fact that the girl wasn't shivering in the slightest.

After about an hour, in which time the sun had travelled a low line across the sky, Anna put her book down on her stomach. I realised I was going to have to stir my Breton bones. In the time it took her to stretch her arms and sit up on her deckchair, she had cheerfully suggested we should go and visit Midoun. Right now. Silence. I thought back to the description of the hotel on the website. The words *less than ten minutes from the town centre* and *perfectly located for your convenience* were coming back like a boomerang to hit us in the face. I personally could have stayed on that beach like that for a hundred more days, peaceful in a screen saver image, but I couldn't find a good way to say so. Anna looked at me with her are-you-really-that-incurious? face. I put my book down too, thinking: This is always how it is on holiday: a constant clash of wills. Above us, clouds were gathering or dispersing, it was hard to tell which, but either way the weather was turning. Happy to put an end to the long spell of inactivity, Rim leaped up and put on her jumper. 'Easy does it,' said Anna, like an old lady; she was going to see if they could hire a car. An hour of respite, I thought. She'd need to go back to the room to look for her passport, find it, come back down and get through to the right person on the phone. But ten minutes later, while Rim was doing stretches and reminding me of a mussel on a barbecue, Anna was already back, telling us there was a white Clio waiting for us out front. 'Come on, let's go.' I swallowed my dismay – better to keep my feelings to myself – and followed her back through the hotel lobby.

Quarter of an hour later, Anna parked, one hand on the wheel, behind a truck full of hanging slabs of meat. She learned to drive on mountain switchbacks; parallel parking abroad is child's play to her. In Midoun, the sand stung our eyes. We walked at random through the streets and I weighed up the risk of being buried in a sandstorm and mummified in this picture postcard.

Inside a shop, Anna's eyes briefly circled over some terracotta ashtrays before landing on a djellaba which seemed properly artisanal, i.e. as if it had really been made out in the remote Tunisian desert. A black dress with colourful fireworks embroidered around the neck. A difficult item to wear in Paris – maybe just to pop out for cigarettes in, when you're spending the day on your own. But God only knows what goes through the heads of human beings who go into tourist shops. She rummaged on the inside of it for the tag, a scrap of card so tiny it was difficult to grab on to. Unable to decipher the number written in pencil, she went and stood in front of the shopkeeper with a colonial smile that said *Finish what you're doing first, I'll wait, of course*, as he finished folding a big woven tablecloth. Then, when he gave her a look that invited her to speak, she asked if what she thought she'd read on the label was indeed the price. Well. Well then, this guy, who must have been about thirty, narrowed his eyes to the point that Anna could no longer see his irises. He seemed to be making some strategic internal calculations. He nodded to say *Yes, yes, that's right, the number you said, that's the price, absolutely*, but his pupils didn't return to the light. A duellists' silence settled between them. Then another customer entered the shop. This woke up the shopkeeper, who set about haggling.

By this point, Anna had figured it out. She knew she was negotiating the dress's serial number, not its price, but she was stuck: the amount they were debating wouldn't have been unreasonable at all in France, and contesting it would have revealed what she had become. A horrible tourist blowing money in the sun. Making a scene would mean interplanetary ridicule. An entry in the shameful annals of neoliberalism. She came to find us near the shop door and, instead of joining in our conversation about the 2009 Rio to Paris plane crash (I had recently reread the official report and was summing up its conclusions for Rim, who couldn't care less), she glanced behind the not-quite-closed curtain into the back of the shop. What she saw there devastated her: an open drawer with a hundred copies of her djellaba in plastic packaging, and the shopkeeper showing its contents to two friends, who were shaking with laughter. A spectacle of her total gullibility. Rim, the whole purchase having totally passed her by, sensed that something was afoot. Her eyes skipped several times from Anna's bag to the back of the shop.

'What's wrong? Tell us, it's easier. You'll never want to set foot here again otherwise.'

Red-faced, Anna told her what had happened – 'But it's okay, it's nothing, no harm done, I'm just a caricature.' I told her: 'It's not that bad. That'll teach us for acting like nineties tourists.' Rim headed for the half-open curtain and pulled it aside with a little jerk. I thought she was going to do something spectacular, like a backflip, but instead she addressed the shopkeeper.

'Hello! I have a question. Do you think my friend is ridiculous?'

'No,' he said, 'but she's no businesswoman!'

The two men who had been laughing coughed.

'And that's a good thing or not, is it, being no businesswoman?' asked Rim, with the grammar of someone who's just finished a boozy lunch.

'It's good,' he said. 'Yes, it's good!' With that, he approached Anna. He looked into her eyes and shook her by the shoulders. 'Yes, of course it's good! People like you make good stories to tell children. What do you think? I'll never forget you! All the other customers from this morning have already left my memory. Not you!'

'And it's nice for us in your memory, is it?' she asked.

'Very comfortable, yes.'

With this reply, I understood that in Anna's head the trip was saved. Thrilled with this story of a djellaba sold for the price of a night in a hotel, the shopkeeper, whose name was Jalil, offered us tea, three pretty red scarves and dozens of spice packets. As we went back to the car, I felt an end-of-the-day tension take over my hands. Tiredness after the journey from Paris, no doubt.

'What does *T* stand for? Rim, what is it?' On each sachet, Jalil had written a letter in red felt tip.

'I don't know. Turmeric, probably.'

'And *F*, fuck, what's *F* for?'

'I don't know, Armelle, you'll have to try it and find out!'

Outside the car, when Anna asked me if I'd rather put the spices in the boot or have them on my lap, I froze. The smell of curry makes my head spin. No one cooks worse than I do. The dishes always seem to find ways to mock me. What I really wanted to do with those spices was to throw them away. I was struck by the absurdity of bringing them in the car, putting them somewhere in the hotel, taking them with me on the plane, the airport shuttle, the Métro and then keeping them in a cupboard for a lifetime. I felt a manic laugh rising in me – I was forced to crouch down to avoid pissing myself. I was laughing so hard, saying, 'I'm never gonna use them,' or rather trying to, that Anna started cracking up too, banging her fist on the roof of the Clio. Already sitting in the back, only Rim was immune to the general hysteria. Happy with her packet of harissa and the adventures in the sun, she was singing 'Ella, elle l'a' by France Gall. '*Ooh ooh ooh-ooh, ooh ooh-ooh.*'

Once we'd calmed down and got in the car, I remembered that Rim had been conceived in 1979 in a Moroccan tent during her parents' honeymoon. I thought about her name, an Arabic word that means antelope or gazelle, I can never remember which – I don't even know if there's a difference – and how her mother had chosen it as an homage to that passionate stay in the desert. For the first time, I thought that despite the gap in her teeth, her natural habitat wasn't Piccadilly Circus but at the top of these dunes. There was something in her that couldn't be seen. The place of her conception and her tastes held secret meetings. I adjusted the rear-view mirror to see her better: she gave me her look of an older sister who knows full well that Armelle means *bear* in Breton, that I'm awkward, blind as a bat, with no taste and a stomach that can't tolerate potatoes. When Anna set off, I said, 'Midoun's nice, but it's dense,' and I suggested we spend the next day in the hotel.

5

Bouvarde and Pécuchette

I met Anna just after leaving journalism school, in July 2008. It was my first job, a temporary contract at a women's magazine. Two years later, we would both be poached at the same time by *Arts*, the culture magazine where our trio was formed. But in the meantime, we worked in deepest darkest Asnières in an old factory built of giant slabs of concrete and workshop windows that got very hot in the middle of the day. Recently broken up with a boy who had gone off to live in Oman, I was living in a studio on Place de Clichy, right on Métro line 13, and my career as a journalist, the curiosity and open-mindedness it involved, was going to pulverise the isolation of my childhood once and for all. The first time I walked into the open-plan office, I saw a young woman sitting cross-legged on the floor reading *L'Humanité*, which struck me as odd. Her dress sense seemed old-fashioned. Later in the day, I caught her name and learned that she was a theatre specialist. Because of the shape of her face and her golden colours, I nicknamed her Romy Schneider for a while. I also picked up on her way of staying on her feet when she was talking to people. Her chest, gigantic by my measure, broke through the rays of dust in the room. As for me, at twenty-eight, the fishing net was long gone. Although my body had the contours of a Vélib' ticket dispenser, I did have some physical qualities. Big red curls and a pretty snub nose. I resembled an unhappy Welsh student, which wasn't so bad.

Sizing Anna up, I thought that we could be friends, but also that friendship couldn't be my priority. First I had to make a place for myself in the heart of the team. 'You have to make yourself indispensable,' they had repeated to us a hundred times at journalism school. (How? By licking people's bodies each morning?) Within two months, I achieved this by agreeing to write about everything, up to and including the boom in transparent umbrellas in Japan. The day a permanent contract landed on my desk, I invited Anna to come and celebrate it with me over a Thai meal. From then on, two-hour lunches reigned supreme. A new stage of friendship was reached in the autumn, when we went out on assignment together. She was driving at night, with the mixtape of a young rapper named Kendrick Lamar playing on repeat (she sang along with a perfect accent, better than his, which seemed strange to me given that she'd grown up in Savoy), when, seeing the fuel gauge going into the red, I cried, 'Careful, we'll have a meltdown!' A long, complicit silence in the front seats. Two smiles directed at the lit-up road, and backlit by its reflection. The hard shoulder was shining on our right and the car was laughing along with us as it swallowed up the road in front. I'd never made such a beautiful slip of the tongue. Anna changed lanes to take the exit on the right. 'You'll realise we're coming off here to avoid having a meltdown – or indeed a breakdown.' She parked up on the verge of the country road and kept smiling as she downloaded the Total app. 'I'm a bad driver but a good compass,' I told her. She slipped me her phone, I guided her through the countryside, and once we were in the cafe of a little service station that seemed to exist just for us and just for that night, we had our first proper conversation about life: 'So, tell me why we can't have a meltdown.'

On our way back to Paris two days later, Anna said to me: 'Before you arrived at the magazine, I'd heard people say that you were a joyful person. When you turned up, I didn't get it at first. But now I really see it.'

'...'

'You have a lovely constancy to your character. It's joyful in a sense.'

Those were still the days when we didn't google everything, and so I didn't have the reflex to go and consult the definition of the word 'joy' in an online dictionary, but I have since and Larousse's definition doesn't mention 'constancy' once.

On the city outskirts, Anna elaborated on the thought, explaining that I gave people a warm psychological welcome: 'The conversation isn't all on your terms.' She also liked how I didn't have any 'drive to improve' them. I tried to understand them, not to correct them. Then she said that the rhythm of my speech was 'like a nice little waltz'. I thanked her, thinking that I would have also liked to be joyful in the traditional sense of the word. But for that I would need medication or the end of my unspecified dread. I nicked three sweets from her packet of Giant Strawbs, chewing them one after the other to give myself time to think of a response, then I said that, first of all, I loved that she had this taste for junk food, which was counter-intuitive in someone so keen on theatre. She smiled as if to say *What are theatre lovers supposed to like?* She'd discovered Haribo at the Annecy multiplex, she told me. The only reason she'd got her driving licence was to take her little sister there on Saturday nights. To get out of Cluses, where 'apart from the Museum of Watchmaking and Turning, there's nothing to do at the weekend'. I admired her unconventional intelligence, I added, afraid that she was annoyed. Her brain seemed to have been better oxygenated than mine, from birth. 'Your thought processes sweep away everything in their path,' I continued. For example: on this trip, I'd lent her a book that was a bit out there. As she gave it back to me, the same morning, she summed it up: 'It's fun, but all it does is add to the distance between us and the world.' I didn't make any comment, but I was impressed by this remark, which reminded me of the similarly definitive one made by Virginia Woolf about a text she deemed disappointing: 'I get no help in judging life.'

As we parted ways that evening, I thought Anna's reason for living was exactly that: to judge this life as much as she could. To exhaust all its possibilities in order to fully possess it. Her understanding of the world was eroticised, and underneath her fifties actress's physique a charming robot was hiding, requiring disks of diverse thought from

61

those around her that it could use to improve its intellectual performance and augment its own reality with what others shared of theirs. Living alongside her meant putting your intelligence in her service: getting sucked in, offering her terrestrial nourishment, transfusing it into her. Giving her human documents, reading recommendations, debriefs on fiction. Experiences and hindsight on your own emotions. All this material was collected to break her interior reclusion, so she could expand her horizons and feel things. Once in the office canteen, I heard her ask a colleague who was about to retire, with no preamble: 'I heard you were depressed when you were younger. Please tell me what that was like.' Followed by: 'What role did female friendship play in your recovery?' *But seriously, how do you do it, all of you – how do you live without grandiosity, without being disappointed by reality?* she seemed to be constantly asking. Once I was home again, I sent her the playlist of classical music she'd asked for that began with Handel's 'Lascia ch'io pianga' ('Let me weep'). Two days later, she wanted another, and I felt the intensity of our bond.

Even when it's like a lightning strike, friendship doesn't develop as quickly as romantic love. It's a gradual process that arrives without warning and comes from afar, from deep in each person's prehistory, where the fondness for one human musicality or another is constructed. But in the present, there is above all a desire to listen as strong as the desire to speak, and this twin desire teleports you from lunchtime to lunchtime, from conversation on the Métro platform to conversation inside the Métro train. At the beginning, it's fragile – you don't know if it's going to synchronise – and then one morning, when you wake up, there's no doubt: there it is. A belt surrounds us, meshing our wheels together. The best of yourself has found a new destination. Now you call each other things like *My little sock* (Anna) or *My koala* (Rim).

I think that after that assignment in Burgundy, Anna and I began the perfect friendship. Each of us, listening to the other, saw the path of our thoughts laid out. We were Bouvarde and Pécuchette, the female counterparts of the protagonists of Flaubert's unfinished novel, *Bouvard et Pécuchet*. Our lives were put in a communal thought fund. I had then had children with Daniel – funny, intellectual, obsessive, separated from his first wife (who had unfortunately remained his best friend-slash-confidante). Anna lived with Panchi and feared his moral perfection. I described the feeling of transgression I got from sleeping with an older man. She told me how her progressive boyfriend wouldn't stop telling her he loved her during sex, which she found distracting. We broached the thorny subject of out-of-sync orgasms: no one talks about it but, in the best-case scenario, a woman has to go from earth-shattering pleasure to the most irritating repetition there is. We talked about age: if it seemed easy to love ourselves at thirty or forty, would we manage it at sixty? We kept a list of women who seemed to have worked it out. At the top of the list, I put a fashion journalist at *Le Figaro* and a painter who made canvases inspired by Nicolas de Staël: two women who know what beauty is. The painter lived in Bréhat in a fisherman's cottage with an orange cement floor. Her studio was hidden away at the bottom of the garden. She wore a navy-blue woolly hat and a natural linen dress and I imagined myself wearing the same thing at that age. *My soft thighs will rub against each other as I go from one room to the other, and it will be perfect.* I'll have a Dalmatian at my heels.

I don't know how it is for men, but intimacy between women is profound. What happens, once we become friends, is that we invite each other into our internal machinery. We introject each other. On the stage of an average day, I seem to be alone: I talk, I eat, I work, I flirt – in that order. But in the wings, many people are happily hard at work with monkey wrenches.

On holiday, I would call Anna: 'Hey girl. I'm on the beach and next to me there's an old couple who are practically having sex on a beach towel. All is not lost.'

'I love that. Tell me about them.'

'They're good-looking and indiscreet. She has grey hair, huge sunglasses and a brick-red vareuse jacket. He could be Louis C.K.'s older brother. Although he's wearing capri pants. I owe you the truth.'

'No big deal, it still sounds great.'

'Yeah. But anyway, I wanted to tell you: let's not *worry* any more, we're going to be fine: our eccentricity will see us through.'

'The party endorses this statement. It's like when I see photos of Charlotte Perriand in old age – her charisma reassures me. I've got faith in the future.'

Like Charlotte Perriand, Anna wore her shirt collars turned up. I still have one clear image in particular of her with her shirt collar like that. It was a morning in autumn 2009 – Daniel's ex-wife's birthday. He was getting ready to go and meet her for coffee. It was still dark and as he was getting dressed, in jeans and a jumper with no top underneath, I pretended to be asleep to contain the jealous misery running through my head. When the door had slammed behind him and just as I was about to start weeping with possessive rage, Anna called me. One year we'd been friends and already she knew exactly the right time to call. Her Twingo was parked outside my building. I pulled on my jeans and ran down the stairs. In the car, her fair hair was pulled back in a bun, her shirt collar turned up, her throat bare. Leather sandals. At my feet she put down a packet of twenty Pasquier pains au chocolat, which we went to eat on the Île de Puteaux, at the top of a concrete slope falling dramatically into the Seine. She snapped away at me with two disposable cameras. We took the road past Disneyland Paris, where *Spider-Man* was showing in 3D. On the way back, Anna and I discussed Daniel's relationship with his ex-wife. 'I'd bet you my arm that they'll be buried next to each other. It's written in the stars – they get on too well and too badly at the same time for it not to be eternal,' I told her, before asking her opinion on the long-term suitability of a tomb for three, with the risk of subterranean vaudeville. I asked more generally where I should be buried. She replied, 'You and the arm you've just lost? In north Brittany, for sure.' We were passing Montmartre cemetery.

She suggested we stop and have a look around, and it was there, in the autumnal atmosphere that makes such places seem almost attractive, while we searched for an empty hundred-year plot near François Truffaut, that she told me about her parents.

They were both posties in Cluses, in Savoy, she began, and posties exactly as you'd imagine them to be: rational, dynamic people. But when she was four, they began constructing a bobsleigh run. Neither of them had ever practised the sport; the crazy idea had come to them as they were watching the Winter Olympics on TV one night. It was two in the morning, there wasn't even any commentary on at that time, when Michel tapped Christine on the leg and she opened her eyes a little wider. 'Couldn't we do that on your family's land?' he asked. After that, they drank their cold tea in a state of real excitement. The uselessness and poetry of the project spoke to a nagging rage against capitalism, Anna told me. The furious desire to do something with the piece of hillside land that had been left to them, their only heritage, did the rest. The following Saturday, her father woke at dawn, pulled on his big brown woollen jumper and went out in search of cheap local materials. For her part, her mother sat at the kitchen table and got stuck into calculations so the bobsleighs wouldn't turn into flying missiles at any of the planned eighteen bends. From then on, Saturdays were dedicated to parts and algebra. Sundays to models. Every summer, luge fanatics they'd met in online forums joined them to help with construction. At the end of August, their departure left a hole. But autumn would come around and

Anna and her sister would contemplate the mandarin peaks, waiting for the first days of winter when that year's work would be tested. The moment of truth. The girls would go down first because they weighed less, and now Anna was a mother herself, the hippy recklessness of that choice filled her with rage. To build the circuit, they used ravine rock and earth, upon which they placed a sophisticated wooden structure. A layer of ice several centimetres thick formed over it on cold nights. The track's construction was going to take a century. 'The last I heard, they're up to ten functioning bends, one of which is 180 degrees,' said Anna.

Once the tunnel was finished, the idea was to make it open to all the children in the area. 'That's nice,' I said, suddenly understanding my friend's obsession with climate change: it wasn't going to ruin just the planet, but also a lifetime of effort. The utopian aspect of the project impressed Anna. And for the most part she would rather imagine her parents working on that than spreading fake news on Facebook. It made them unique. She also admired her father's physical strength – he was undertaking a real feat. It was a grounded, noble and very hands-on enterprise. But on the other hand, she could see that these two sexagenarians were as off their rockers as the stars of her old *Guinness World Records* book. Weren't they megalomaniacs, in the psychiatric meaning of the word? She and her little sister had spent their whole childhoods hearing them go on about the tunnel ('Michel, what time are we going down to the bob track tomorrow?'). Since she had been working in Paris, Anna only went back there for short visits. Exasperation mounted quickly. By the third day, she'd be looking to the heavens and asking herself under her breath what the symbolic meaning of this Bob was, this virile presence who dictated their entire existence. By the end of the trip, she allowed herself to be harsher in her criticisms. Her parents treated her like a 'bougie Parisian in the pocket of the mainstream media'.

'They love me as long as I support the project,' she said.

'That's a start,' I said.

On Truffaut's tomb, which we and a fat grey cat were keeping warm with our bums, I told her about Rim, who she didn't know yet, and her mother, whose love was also dependent on certain criteria. Now, as Daniel opens the bedroom curtains in a theatrical manner, though still without managing to distract me, I think back to that conversation about parental failings and begin to understand our dark side. Anna and I clairvoyantly calculated the time we had left to live. The impossibility of forgetting our mortality, even for a second, put us in a state of despair. 'The hourglass is running out,' she would often say, and it's true that, as members of a hard-to-please people, suffering from an indefinable absence (the desire for a desire that doesn't rest on anything), our tolerance for a neutral, benign sort of happiness was about ten minutes. We were like two bags of rice hanging in a warehouse, emptying out grain by grain. The feeling of loss was constant and painful, our outlook on life like that of two sisters isolated in the English countryside, two old maids, seeing their wrinkles deepening every evening in the candlelight. With the sound of an egg boiling for a soundtrack.

To forget that death was already circulating noisily in our bloodstreams, we sought out immersive experiences. Psychoanalysis, twice a week, and writing, which we did on Sundays, took us to the heart of the focal point of concentration which allows you to escape elsewhere. She wrote plays; I wrote screenplays. Love also offers an escape. Passion is a psychoactive drug that alters your hormonal balance, heart rhythm, neural pathways, facial symmetry and body temperature – it changes your perception of reality, which becomes sublime.

6

The Man with the Date Essential Oils

The all-you-can-eat breakfast at the Djerba Azur was reason enough on its own to have visited. We returned to the suite happy and full of yogurt, and waited for the outside temperature to rise. Sitting on the floor, Anna and I were amusing ourselves looking through the Tunisian Monopoly set we'd discovered under the sofa – Champs-Élysées becomes Avenue Habib Bourguiba – when Rim rushed out of the bathroom with her jeans still undone. Her post-pregnancy belly showed no apparent signs of trauma. She had just received a private message on Instagram composed entirely of sentences in the present participle, which she then recited impressively. *Brushing your hand in the lift. Watching you walk along the shore. Wanting to speak to you so badly.* Something along those lines. Huddled around her phone as if it were a smoking engine, we observed that this romantic message had been sent seven minutes earlier by a certain Raphaël.

We recognised him despite the filters on his profile picture: it was the man in his forties with the firm buttocks and the Ricard bucket hat we'd noticed the day before on the beach. We'd seen him again that morning by the crêpe stand at breakfast, an hour earlier. My attention had been caught by his little boy, about five years old, who was going around all the tables and leaving a feeling of unease in his wake. I had to get closer to understand. It was very simple: the kid was stopping to say 'shukran' (pronounced 'shook-ran') to all the non-white people in the restaurant. In other words: because he had misunderstood a pleasantry, he was going round thanking all the 'racialised' guests in the hotel, with the slight impatience all glasses-wearing little boys have to boot. The hurt on an Indian man's face made my stomach twist, and I looked over at Raphaël who, pioneering the 'I don't know this weird kid' strategy, was stirring his coffee and looking through the bay window at the four swimming pools.

In the bedroom, Rim zipped up her jeans.

'Aside from the firmness of his arse, we know nothing about him.'

What now? She let the information sink in for ten seconds, then she said we should launch a coordinated investigation into his online presence. Like a NASA mission (more like a Google mission really). The idea was quite funny and that's what we would have done, lying on our fronts on the double bed, if the guy hadn't had a Wikipedia page that I found straight away. It was an embryo of a page, five paragraphs and two footnotes, but it still made up the picture of a man. Thanks to that, we knew everything. Even the fact that he'd come top of his class at his very prestigious university.

'Aha! That's a detail which suggests he's edited his own page,' I said.

'You have no way of knowing that,' Rim replied.

'Admit that there's a chance.'

'There's a chance.'

Before our eyes unfurled the bibliography of a young writer specialising in lyrical portraits of downtrodden women. Mistreated, abandoned, undone: all from different eras. At first glance (titles and summaries), it didn't seem like he wanted to bring them back to life or find justice for them but to fix them in the pain of their time and their condition. 'He's the kind of man who wouldn't have done anything for his heroines at the time but gets a thrill imagining that he would,' I said. I was all the more angry because I know this feeling: journalists are not the last to use the misfortune of others to boost their own egos. The undercurrent of suffering and the writer's revelling in it are entwined in the kinds of sentences that send me wild. Our profession rewards those who write lyrical pieces about a farmer crushed by her own cow, or an artist who dies in a car crash, and the line between reporting a tragedy and blowing your own trumpet is incredibly fine. One thing doesn't deceive: pathos. The question we must ask ourselves is as follows: does the article have any tangible consequences other than the immediate improvement of its author's image? Good question.

I said: 'That's the kind of guy who dips his pen in other people's wounds.'

Rim didn't reply.

'He'll end up as a presenter on France Culture, you'll see.'

Rim didn't bat an eyelid.

'He's not as nice as Niels, physically.' Her daughter's father is a man who cuts planks of wood topless in the park while listening to Norwegian metal – he's unrivalled. I insisted: 'There's no way he knows how to put together a wardrobe.'

No reaction. Her persistent silence made me realise we were going to be saddled with this guy, his cashmere sweaters and his well-received books for the foreseeable future. Rim would say she was done with silent, sporty guys. She would tell us: 'From the start, I needed the opposite. Niels and I are too alike, I need someone who'll ask existential questions.' (That is to say, someone who'll split hairs endlessly.) Upon finding a ridiculous photo of Raphaël behind a turntable, his hands in the air, I added that he DJed for parties sponsored by Huawei. But no one acknowledged receipt. Anna was smiling indulgently at Rim, who was describing the 'romantic locks of hair' (by which she meant wavy) she had seen poking out from under his bucket hat the day before on the beach (while he was looking at the young girl). After a long discussion over whether she should also reply using only the present participle, it was decided that no, she would conjugate. Rim arranged to meet him beside the sunniest pool in the Djerba Azur at 3 p.m. She added that we would come with her. Overly focused on our goal, too quick to do all the other activities planned in between, we arrived twenty minutes early. The wind wrinkled the surface of the pool; the deckchairs made a noise like we were in a sailing club. I sat down on a big, misplaced exercise ball and thought about the spices I was going to have to pretend to forget in the hotel room safe the day we left. In a murmur, Rim ordered us to feign a casual conversation. I stood up too quickly and threw my head back laughing. When I brought it down again and the stars I was seeing faded, everything about the guy approaching us irritated me: his unkempt hair, his last-season Ray-Bans, his wireless headphones (since when was a wire so inconvenient?) and his sluggish gait of an aristocrat whose survival reflexes have been genetically deactivated by generations of comfort. 'Hello girls,' he said in English. He took off his hoodie, letting us glimpse how prominent his belly button was, and carried on, looking at Rim: 'I know who you are. I often read your columns.'

'You're an online subscriber?' asked Rim.

'No, I buy it in print.'

'Oh! I didn't realise you were eighty-five years old.'

'I hesitated before messaging you this morning because I think we should never meet the people we like to read. I'm surely going to be disappointed by your conversation...'

Once he was lying on one of the plastic deckchairs, Raphaël spread his bony legs as if to make sure no one could come and sit next to him. Then he applied sun cream to his torso, making weird little circles around his nipples with his finger. As he did so, he told Rim he'd come to Tunisia to finish his sixth book. 'Why the Azur?' (He was asking himself the question.) Because he'd realised by chance, two

years earlier, that literary inspiration struck best while he
was being massaged in the Blue Ocean Institute with date
essential oils. Really. He said those actual words. I rolled
my eyes, horrified. Anna must have been too, since she was
nervously brushing down the insides of her thighs. To stop
myself from screaming, I reminded myself that overheard
conversations are never easy on the ear. (Perhaps because
the spy doesn't catch the nuances that give them secret
depths. Or – the most pessimistic hypothesis I believe in
– because human conversations are often low-quality and
we only block our critical gaze when it comes to our own.)
I also tried to remember a debate between Flaubert and
Nietzsche, summarised somewhere by Houellebecq, on the
psychomotricity of writing. Flaubert claims that one only
thinks and writes well while sitting down, while Nietzsche
believes that anything not conceived of while walking
is worthless. As for Houellebecq, he thinks that walking
calms the interior conflicts arising from the ideas that jostle
about during the writing phase. Sitting down, that is. And
then there was Raphaël, who wrote lying down and doused
in fruit oils.

Because Rim insisted (lending an uncharacteristic light-
ness to her voice as she said it) on knowing the subject of
his next book, Raphaël ended up telling her that he was
currently working on a portrait of Madame de Montespan,
Louis XIV's abandoned mistress. He was giving himself
until the end of the holiday, so another five days, to
describe how she felt when the king eventually fell in love
with a young girl of seventeen and she was banished to an

attic in the chateau. Listening to him, I thought it would be better to be one of those inept, overly literal writers who visit Versailles eight times to immerse themselves than this obscene weirdo. *Can you write about anything you want from a five-star hotel?* Yes, but no you can't, for fuck's sake. May the ghost of Madame de Montespan murder this over-cultured prick with a pickaxe, I thought as he described his writing routine. Every morning, Raphaël dropped his son off at the Kids Club. He would then return to his room, slide on his foam flip-flops and his thick robe with the Azur branding, tuck a spiral notebook and a hotel pencil inside his swimming trunks and head very slowly towards the spa. Inside cabin forty-four, his favourite, his body turned to jelly and his grey matter was activated. That morning, he had noted down an interesting phrase: *The solitude of the witness.* Among these absurd details, which somehow impressed her nonetheless, Rim learned the fundamentals: Raphaël was divorced from a woman named Kim, who worked in film and knew the actor Pierre Niney well.

'She loved me against my nature,' said Raphaël.

'I see,' Rim replied.

'She wanted me to love her. That was her goal. That I wouldn't cheat on her, that I'd belong to her. It was only about her, really. She was obsessed with what she meant to me.'

'Yes.'

'What I need is the opposite: a gentle woman who wants the best for me. Even if that means it's not so passionate.'

'Of course, that's normal.'

I know Rim well enough to know that she doesn't find that normal at all. She looks down on the kind of men who want to live like a pig in clover, never challenged intellectually. That evening we ate in our suite, on the sofa, going over the historical period covered in Raphaël's book; everything that happened before 1914 is, unfortunately, a bit vague for the three of us. Then we brushed our teeth together with a silly game of looking at each other in the mirror, because nothing makes me laugh more than observing the dexterity, fervour and sheer intensity of concentration which Rim brings to brushing her teeth (she's unleashed; it's like *Jurassic Park* in the bathroom twice a day).

To pick up the thread of this story, which seems very distant this morning, my friend lost the upper hand the minute our plane touched down in France.

First, there was the so-called 'moral phase' imposed by Raphaël: so as not to destroy her relationship with Niels, the writer refused to see her in Paris ('it's too dangerous, we won't be able to set boundaries'), but he sent her thirty-three texts per day anyway. They would stick to written communication, and those conversations, as frequent as they were, wouldn't condemn them in court, he argued. In the eyes of the law, yes, it was all clean. What he carefully omitted was that in the eyes of the heart, something was definitely going on. And through the constant *What are you up to?* and *How are you doing?* texts, this guy was occupying my friend's thoughts more and more. Two months and three false alarms of a meeting later, Raphaël inexplicably U-turned and asked Rim to come to his and bring something for lunch. *I'd rather warn you in advance, I'm not going to cancel our date for once*, he'd sent her late that morning. Rim's heart skipped two beats. The invitation convinced my friend that he was falling for her when really all it should have told her was that his fridge was empty.

Although Rim's arms were laden with a brown paper bag full of fresh pasta, harissa and macarons, she managed to ring the doorbell. He lived in the Ternes neighbourhood, and boasted a perfectly clean, open-plan kitchen. She made the lunch, afraid to dirty the surfaces, while he spoke to someone called Élodie on the phone. Towards 4 p.m., after having cooked, eaten, cleaned up and fucked on the living-room rug, she left with the impression that the forbidden nature of the situation had turned Raphaël on more than her body, which he had described in the midst of the action as having 'low hips'. (That comment makes my head spin. Low compared to what?) But since his book on Madame de Montespan was being edited and he needed something to do, the messages doubled in intensity. Weeks went past where Rim lied to Niels to go and spend TV-spaghetti-whisky evenings with her lover (evenings she found extraordinary, declaring that she'd found her soulmate). Then, in an attempt to push the relationship further, Rim invited him to see the Paris Philharmonic in concert, during which she was forced to admit that he coughed in the interludes.

After the concert, Raphaël no longer texted her except with closed messages, lacking questions or follow-ups, and always with a slightly more ambivalent tone than hers. The reluctant yielding of a lethargic teenager. This gave Rim the sense that the conversation could be reanimated when in fact no, it was already at an end. She would always send the last message (with, after eleven minutes, that sad *game over* feeling). He'd initiated the step backwards. Pressed the exit button. The goal: to break it off with no drama and, if possible, no conversation. The mistake: like so many before him, Raphaël had made the grave error of thinking that recent mothers make fun mistresses, when actually, once you get close to forty, no one's laughing any more. The potential to destroy the family hangs over everything. Feeling suddenly older than they expected, some women become more vulnerable and intense, and with Raphaël in withdrawal mode, I saw my friend clinging to the threshold between heroism and misery. Overthinking his polite gestures, accepting the sexual turn the relationship had taken without batting an eyelid, persuading herself she didn't want anything more either, and in addition starting to judge her partner as 'slow on the uptake'. Raphaël loved music, like her. He loved 'Something' by the Beatles, like her. How could she have lived, even for a second, with a man who didn't love 'Something' by the Beatles as much as they did? One evening, at her house, while Niels was bathing their daughter, Rim told me she wanted to break up with him as if he was nothing more than a ski instructor she'd fucked twice among the pines. 'I'm over it,' she said, exhaling CBD, which she'd been smoking continuallypi since we got back from Djerba. I was as high as she was, and, scared by my own cruelty, replied: 'Go on then, dump him, you're right. He'll find a nice vegan girl and they'll go climbing in the Dolomites.' Witchy cackles, but I was the one who was afraid. Two days later, while she was making preparations to rent a one-bed (the bedroom was for Aloïs, she'd sleep in the living room until she could find something better), her lover broke up with her in the Jardin des Tuileries before they'd even got to the famous reclining chairs.

'Sorry, Rim, but it won't work for me if you're not with your husband any more.'

'We're not married,' she replied, but that didn't seem to alter his reasoning.

'You know what I mean.'

'No, I don't.'

'I didn't sign up for this. It was supposed to stay casual.'

'You're ditching me because I'm renting a studio?'

'That's the first step. You'll want more.'

'What do you know? I already wanted a space to myself before I met you.'

'I was on board for a fling, not for moving in together. I can hardly believe that I'm having to explain myself. You're the one in a relationship, I should remind you – I don't owe you anything.'

My friend looked at him as if she'd never seen someone so stupid in all her life, something she excels at. She turned on her heel and walked away, aiming for the Luxor Obelisk. Rim never cries, but her eyes mist up and she falls over from emotion. And it was at the foot of the monument, lit up fuchsia in the dusk, that she collapsed like a Spanish widow. Sitting on the floor, she called me, whispering in a terrible voice:

'Hello, Armelle, are you there? Raphaël broke up with me, an hour ago. I'm in the middle of a desolate scene. Le Crillon is crying. The park gate is crying. Even the Métro, going under the street here, is moaning. I swear it's true.' Draw on a cigarette.

'And you, are you crying?'

Exhalation. 'No, I'm not. But everything looks blurry, come and get me please.'

Night was falling, I was watching a Japanese film and it was cold outside. I put on my eldest son's gloves, far too small for me, and took the Métro to Place de la Concorde. I wondered how someone as sporty as her could smoke. Under the arcades of Rue de Rivoli, in a secluded leather booth in an old cafe, the waiter permitted her to light up with a tilt of his head. Her TGV-grey eyes were moist, her hands shaky; she huskily told me that just yesterday Raphaël had asked her to bring him shells from the Normandy beach she was on.

'How much of a pervert do you have to be to dump a woman with shells in her pocket?'

'A huge pervert,' I said, even though I don't like to corrupt psychological terms like that. I added: 'Well, Rim, I have to tell you something.'

'What?'

'You remember how many times you told him to read those Éluard poems? He never did. People like that are—'

'Ungenerous? You're right, but I don't care.'

'You don't care, but it's important.'

'You mean he wasn't really interested in me? Shit, well

help me out then. What's the difference between what I've just gone through and a proper relationship?'

'A proper relationship can unfold. That's all.'

Silence. That definition had surprised us both with its simplicity. Then, with a reproachful note in her voice, Rim asked me what I would do, then, with all the other relationships. Those that don't have the means to unfold. The aborted ones, the thwarted ones, the forbidden ones, the unthinkable ones. Would I throw them all away?

'I'm pleased that they exist, because they prove the value of the former.'

'Were you a priest in a previous life?'

'No, and I'm not necessarily against affairs either. I'm just saying that it being impossible isn't as great as it may seem. It's a stimulation of the senses with no outlet. In the end, you'll explode.'

'Ugh, you're a pain.'

'No, Rim, listen to me. It's just because there's no otherness in these kinds of relationships, that's what makes it feel so good.'

'It doesn't feel *good*, it feels insane.'

'Yes, because there's mutual excitement and overestimation. You flicker, become immortal. But it can only last for a little while and leads you into all manner of mistakes. Your daughter is still so young.'

'I should never have mentioned the studio, that's what made him freak out.'

'And then you'd have kept him for what, another month? One month extra will extend the heartbreak by three more months. It's like with dogs, you have to multiply everything by three.'

'With dogs it's by seven.'

'Oh. Are we sure?'

After a while, I realised Rim would do her best to make sure this conversation never ended. Her goal: to put off going home because home, since that afternoon's break-up, had become the site of defeat. The place where reality had triumphed. The regional terminus of life. The trenches of Verdun on a November day. The decline of the body. The ringing silence that follows Ravel's *Boléro*. Niels's flat-as-a-pancake conversation, his weights in the hallway, his energy bars everywhere and the boiler that turns itself off for no reason.

'What does it really matter if he didn't read Éluard?'

'It was a purely narcissistic love, one that didn't require him to step outside himself at all. A love that aspired solely to receive, to take. A love without generosity.'

'You talk like a guru.'

'Like a therapist, I'd prefer. You were good for him as an object, but you were nothing more than that to him.'

'That's nice, thanks.'

'Could he have been your best friend?'

'No.'

'Then it's wasted time.'

It was 10 p.m. when she took the twenty seashells out of her coat pocket. She piled them up on the cafe table and started explaining her reasoning for choosing each of them, showing them to me one after the other, like an exhibition curator. Hellish. Even more so since dry seashells aren't interesting at all and so, to convey her enthusiasm to me, she had to make the effort to mentally put them back in the sea again. I ordered a menthe à l'eau, thinking that now I was over thirty, one alcoholic drink less would make all the difference in the morning. Then I started in again.

'Tell yourself that the really out-of-the-ordinary love affairs can take their time. Like that Camus quote about friendship: "There are friendships that last and those that don't. The ones that last are the good ones, it's as simple as that."'

'You think this relationship could happen later on?'

'A relationship ends when we die.'

Now I was finally going in the same direction as her brain in its state of withdrawal, leaning towards hope, Rim smiled at me. Then her lips tightened. She said that she knew me well enough to know I wasn't going to stop there, on that optimistic note. I was going to insist that she still had to forget the whole thing because you always end up hating the other person when they've forced a relationship. That you can't build anything on a judo hold. Blah, blah, blah. She knew all my ideas.

'Exactly. I have a Buddhist saying for the occasion.'

'Wait, I bet it's something like: *Do not pull on the tree's branches for its fruit, but wait for it to ripen and fall?*'

'That's it! But whatever happens, Rim, be careful of that "I don't owe you anything". There are people who say things that are technically or legally true but emotionally false.'

'What's that supposed to mean?'

'That he uses language in bad faith. He always shifts the blame, he makes dialectical manoeuvres away from feelings and towards the civil code.'

'Because, according to you, he did owe me something?'

'Yes, of course. I believe we have a responsibility towards the people who love us.'

'Up to what point?'

'Up until they don't love us any more.'

That night, on Rue de Rivoli, Rim kept talking until five in the morning, when the cafe closed. She went from Raphaël's romantic rejection, triggered by 'that fucking studio apartment', to her mother's incapability of loving her as an independent being, back and forth between the two subjects. I hope I managed to help her the way she's helped me at crucial moments in my life. Because it's clear to me that since our meeting in the garden in Neuilly, she's always been a good big sister.

7

The Potato

Rim has been there, been central, at the two most dramatic moments of my life. The first took place in 1990, the weekend my parents separated. I was ten years old. One Saturday morning, my mother, Rim and I went to pick up the keys to my mother's cousin's empty apartment in front of the Sainte-Odile church by the Porte de Champerret. The brick bell tower looked like something out of Gotham City, and it was raining so hard the insides of our ears were wet. The cousin was wearing a raincoat and a beige detective's hat. It wasn't a divorce but an escape. Back in Neuilly, Rim helped us pack the boxes. She applied herself, putting a hundred times as many items in each box as I did. Then, when everything was done, she got in the back seat of my mother's Citroën with its sunroof and we left the neighbourhood, after waving wildly at the statue of the Duke of Orléans. That evening, we ordered dim sum, watched *Pretty Woman* on VHS and slept on mattresses on the floor. My mother and I would live in Belleville from then on, and after a life in the suburbs the tumult of Paris gave me the feeling of my visual diet having switched from prehistoric to digital.

On the Sunday evening of that first weekend, while we were getting ready to take Rim back to Neuilly, I saw a weird drunk guy in front of our new building. He pounced on me. He grabbed me by the arm and pushed me onto the back seat of a dark red Espace with its front door covered in Sellotape. My mother hadn't come down yet. The man, whose face I've forgotten, slammed the door behind me with an otherworldly force, got behind the wheel and set off. I sat up and, through the windscreen, I saw Rim, saw the spark of decision in her eyes. Spreading her arms wide, she stood firm in front of the car, which braked a metre from her feet. She looked as though she was going to climb onto the bonnet. I opened the car door and ran. So did Rim, behind me. I yelled unintelligible words. I heard my mother shout my name. Passers-by were frozen to the pavement. The Espace disappeared around the street corner. The motiveless kidnapping had failed, the madman was never found, and I still have nightmares about it. Sellotape has given me a feeling of imminent death ever since. As a young girl, I never managed to thank Rim for her bravery. I felt oddly annoyed that she'd allowed herself to change the course of my life in so dramatic a manner. Thought at the same time 'Thank you' and 'Mind your own business, for God's sake'.

My second 'drama' took place in 2002. I was twenty-two. I woke up at dawn in my studio in Lille, close to my journalism school. It was 6.45 a.m. and I was killing time in the bath, i.e. feeling my stomach and regularly adding hot water with my feet. I turned on the radio and, at the end of a newsflash I was barely listening to, I heard that there had been a fire overnight outside Belleville Métro station. I was catapulted out of the water. I was naked in the hallway, in the kitchen. Unwillingly naked in the kitchen, in the living room. I sat on the sofa. My laptop vibrated on my damp thighs. Underneath my buttocks, it was soaked. I searched on the internet for the precise location of the fire. I was shaking. The number of my building was cited on *Le Parisien*'s website. I read the article. Someone had jumped out of the window, and I thought that was the kind of thing my mother would do in such a situation. I called her. She didn't pick up. I called again. No answer. There was no further doubt in my mind that it was her who had jumped. Finally, my phone rang. Karine, Rim's aunt, told me she'd been located in the Bichat hospital. When that woman was awake, she was really awake.

That morning, I boarded a train to Paris with no ticket. I stayed standing for the whole journey. A ticket inspector went to give me a fine, but stopped when she saw my face. In the hospital room, an unfamiliar, rasping voice that came from my mother's throat asked me to go and pick up the 'important things'. I pretended to understand. In the apartment, I took at random her new computer, her costume jewellery and her Ventilo scarves. I breathed in the smell of ashes. The next day, when I went to see her, she had been placed in an induced coma. 'It's double or nothing,' said the doctor. 'Double,' I said without knowing if that was the right answer. When I left the little 'family room' he'd taken me into, I saw Rim's back in a beige plastic chair. Which she didn't leave from then on. Every morning, when I arrived on the ward at eight o'clock, she was there in her jogging bottoms. Then one lunchtime, I went to the brasserie on the corner with her. When I saw her eating, hunger came back to me. I started to put my sadness into words. I said that it was too soon to only have a father. That my mother was my only unconditional relationship. That without those connections, you never take any more risks, you get stuck: 'When I was little, I was so afraid of losing her that I was scared another woman in disguise had taken her place in my bed, to tuck me in. I would check the details on her neck.' Rim didn't say that she already knew this story, or that this kind of personal anecdote made her a bit uncomfortable. I stole a potato sprinkled with parsley from her plate and, as if it were the most natural thing in the world, as if it were something that had been decided when she ordered her food, she pushed all the potatoes to my side. A pile of fried carbohydrates, within my reach. All that was left for her was a bit of old, browned lettuce. It was a primitive gesture of pure love. I swallowed it all without saying anything. The best of her salad. Then we went back to the hospital.

After the break-up in the Jardin des Tuileries, Rim's sadness lasted until she got a physical wake-up call. One day while she was writing her column, sitting on the wheeled chest in her living room, and more specifically while she was search-ing for a synonym for the word 'say' and pressing her right cheek, she discovered a little solid lump under her fingers. In the exact place where Raphaël had one. A mimicry cyst. On her face. She charged into the bathroom, hollering. Then she called her Russian auriculotherapist, Evgeny, a man who knows nothing about MRIs. He massages your earlobes, says something ambiguous and invariably prescribes vitamin tablets, but Rim likes him and always leaves her sessions with him with a better understanding of herself. After the appointment, she messaged me to say that she'd realised Raphaël had never loved her as much as she'd imagined: *I've had it with loving him on my own.* Then Anna and I received a voice note: 'At least once a year, we should get access to a counter tracking the time someone has spent thinking about us. That would avoid lots of misunderstandings, don't you think?'

She followed that with a Genesis song she was loudly singing in the street, among the cars. First the intro (*'Dum, dum, dum, dum, dum'*), and then the lyrics, in which the outraged singer says there must be some kind of mistake: he was waiting in the rain for hours and the girl never arrived. I listened to 'Misunderstanding' twice on YouTube and replied that the kind of people who make others wait in the rain end up in the middle of cemeteries, in unfindable tombs. And that the cyst would disappear with the Russian's medications. And, in any case, the only people who say cysts don't disappear naturally after a while are surgeons with nothing to do in August. I also sent her 'Heartbreak Hotel' by Whitney Houston: *Look, she knew how to get back on top.*

After closing the double door of her healer's building behind her, Rim grabbed her phone and texted Niels to suggest they meet up for a coffee.

Where are you?

Near the Champs, at my ear guy's.

I'm on my way.

As my childhood friend went back to her shy, sporty Norwegian, while they celebrated their reconciliation with the purchase of a grand piano and new climbing ropes, while their apartment ceased to be a realm of boredom and impatience, a place of withdrawal where you wander around like you've lost something unspecified, basically while family life stopped tasting like sand and Rim's brain was back to normal, Anna and I were still in the depths of the romantic abyss.

*

It's almost 10 a.m. this 23 May. Daniel knocks on our bedroom door, opens it a crack.

'Just wondering, are you planning on getting up today?'

'No.'

8

The Myth of Proteus

To understand Anna's debacle, we have to go back to the beach in Tunisia, on 24 December, where we were waiting in an ironic way for the Christmas festivities to start, alongside thirty or so other people. A little way off, on an overhang on the dune, a Tunisian with an angular face and pale eyes was smoking a cigarette as he scanned the crowd with an air of immense interior distance. Without thinking, Anna took a glass of orange juice from the buffet and brought it to him. It was a strange, almost unsettling initiative, but the man, who was about forty, thanked her. She asked if he was staying at the hotel and he shook his head mockingly. His name was Adel and he'd come to support his brother, who the Azur had hired to play one of the Three Wise Men in the show that was about to start. He didn't have time to elaborate further because the music began to crackle – 'Silent Night' was playing through two speakers sunk into the sand – and we saw, arriving on camelback from the end of the beach, three young men swathed in Aladdin costumes. The Wise Men pointed at the sky, miming the tricky business of navigating by the stars (the star of Bethlehem, which announced the birth of Jesus to Melchior, Caspar and Balthazar, also guided them towards Jerusalem). But as the sky that day was absolutely blue, the kind of blue there's no need to even describe, the scene was pathetic. The three men seemed to be saying to each other: *Well, if there were a cloud up there, maybe we wouldn't be so hot.*

Adel's little brother looked like him and he was riding the biggest camel – perhaps also the most senile, since its mouth produced a continuous noise like a bathtub draining (but I'm no camel expert). After a while, the three animals came to a stop on an imaginary line. Some of the hotel guests then rushed to take selfies with them and get up in the saddle in turn. Others carried on dancing about barefoot to the music. After 'Silent Night', 'Jingle Bells' came on, followed by 'Last Christmas', written by George Michael, incongruous in a country where homosexuality was still illegal. I saw that Anna wanted to console Adel about all this kitschiness. Approaching them, I heard her apologise on behalf of the West and him assure her that it was okay. He had also played a Wise Man to pay for his tourism studies in Tunis, and had taken it up again later. Anna carried on assailing him with personal questions, which he only answered because he thought she was hot. He spoke six languages and ran guided tours of the Berber villages built into the rock in the desert. Opposite his own, which was called Chenini, there was a big rock which she might have seen in a *Star Wars* film. Did she know the one he was talking about?

'No. I saw them when I was little.'

'Shame, because it's the highlight of my village.'

'As a guide' (he started several sentences with that), Adel hoped Chenini would be able to live entirely off tourism one day. Recently, he'd had the idea of selling desert roses at the entrance to the village, which was going well. But not everything was moving in the right direction: the plastic bottles littering every street corner, dropped by foreigners and Tunisians alike, made him want to scream at the hills. The parasol attack had reduced numbers. Deep down, he knew he didn't have the patience for this kind of work. One day, he had yelled at a father who refused to take a photo of the most spectacular view, from above, of his village. Adel and the German, who had already taken 1,463 photos under duress, came to blows over it. Summoned by the mayor of Chenini-Nahal, the municipality covering the two neighbouring villages, Adel had exclaimed, at the end of the meeting, that no holiday slide show was complete without Chenini. He was immediately ashamed of this crazy declaration. Leaving the town hall, he had gone to sit in the middle of the football pitch drawn in the sand below the village. 'You did a quick bit of psychoanalysis,' said Anna. 'Not really, no. I don't believe in that sort of thing,' he replied. My friend was staring at the opening of his linen shirt, where a scar ran across his neck. Seeing Adel straighten up like someone who's getting ready to leave, she asked if she could come to Chenini to see his goats before we went back to France. She would compare his to the ones in Savoy, they would have lots to discuss. He agreed, stubbing out his cigarette on the edge of his shoe. In the meantime, Adel's little brother had transformed into Father Christmas. He was distributing toys imported from China which wouldn't last longer than the time it took to give them out. Plastic fell noiselessly onto the sand and most of the children were crying.

The next day, Rim and I waited for Anna for hours, in the empty restaurant in Chenini. I was in a bad mood. We ate an enormous plate of couscous while watching Tunisian TV, and drank cup after cup of mint tea until we felt sick. I bought postcards of the *Star Wars* rock, thinking of my sons.

Once we were back in France, Anna's relationship with Adel was consolidated by them sending videos of their daily lives to each other. Her of the outside of the Gare de Lyon, him of his village. I imagine Adel held out for a long time against the idea of falling in love with a girl who gets news alerts on her phone and uses the word 'libido' once every three sentences. But at the end of the day, as Anna's curiosity about him was real, persistent, deep and flattering, a trapdoor was opened. For her part, my friend was smitten. She loved that his physical strength was equal to her father's, that he lived surrounded by that ochre colour, and that he didn't oblige her, like the 'bourgeois Parisians' did, to live beyond her sociocultural means. She liked his long scar. One day, at the office, Anna received a letter written in Arabic. Adel was inviting her to join him in a cave in Chenini. As Panchi was away filming a documentary in South America, the coast was clear. She bought her plane ticket. In a hollow in the rock, Adel had put down a bed and made a trail of candles towards it. That evening, he and Anna were in agreement about everything. Profoundly relaxed, Adel saw the plastic bottles differently: he put them in his ears to do a Yoda imitation. Then he read her poetry, and Anna loves it when you're able to change register like that.

However, the sexual tension only lasted until Adel came to Paris to visit her in turn. At which point: fizzle. Far from home, he wasn't the same. Especially on the Métro. It was like his charm had been extinguished. This failed trip made Anna go distant, which her lover seemed to put up with until the day he disappeared. Phone number: changed. No response over email. Even though she didn't think she loved him any more, Anna found this ghosting deeply traumatic. Up until our trip to Brittany, she was still asking me why she hadn't gone to live with Adel in the desert (aside from the difficulties this would pose for her daughter's education). She would fall into a vortex of perplexity.

'Armelle, I'm spiralling. I can't seem to put myself in the shoes of the girl who wanted to break up with him any more. Help me find her again.'

'How?'

'I don't know, just do it! Led by Love what shall not friendship do?'

'Well then, if we're quoting Racine, I think Racine would say: *Remember how you couldn't stand the way he criticised the noise of Paris.* It's for the best.'

'Why?'

'Because he seemed like a sad guy who you'd have to take care of.'

'And that's not good?'

'Not to live with, no.'

Repeating this phrase for the thousandth time, I prayed that one day they'd invent a post-break-up chatbot, a concept that will one day make a fortune for someone who can code. The principle would be simple: a chatbot capable of sending consoling messages to the person who's been dumped, messages that have already been verified as effective within the context of real-life friendships. Well put together, these messages would be sent in reply to the repetitive questions that lovesick despair produces (in general, variations on 'what was I for him/her?') that their friends just can't take any more. It will take over from humans and their limited patience. The machine will have hundreds of arguments in store that it will send even in the middle of the night, and which affirm the break-up, soothe the pain and build the ego back up. *He was scared of you because you were too intelligent. He was so emotionally immature. He couldn't bear the crazy desire you sparked in him. If you went for such a stupid guy, it was because, deep down, you wanted to keep your family together.* Basically, ego boosts on tap. Strategic instructions: *Don't make any more moves until Wednesday.* Rationalising ones: *Remember that the guy's mother was always tracking him on Find My Friends!* In Anna's case, to be precise, the chatbot could have reminded my friend that even if Adel had been an occupant of what she called her 'house of desire', he'd never have passed the reality check. *Imagine you, him and your daughter in a twenty-mile traffic jam – how would that go?*

Or taught her that Freud defined desire as 'a hallucinatory cathexis of the memory of gratification': see, that's always good to know. At some point, the machine could also have sent her this quote from Frédéric Berthet: 'There are no feelings more overwhelming than those we don't truly feel.' Or this, from David Lynch: 'The things that you imagine are much more beautiful than reality. You know that, right?' Or this one from Nicolas Grimaldi: 'Nothing is more improbable or more phantasmic than expecting the musicality of our lives to come from one person.'

The chatbot would make her relive Adel's trip to Paris in detail, hour by hour. The engine would reply to Anna – who would have asked it if their relationship could be revived – that no, it couldn't, that when it comes to love it's unfortunately not possible to give it a 'simplification shock'. No Etch A Sketch shake. Finally, this excellent resource could remind her of the Greek myth of Proteus, the guardian of the mythical seals who carry the acrid smell of the sea depths. A being with the power to transform himself into a maned lion, a dragon or a leopard to evade the demands of the other characters in the tale. He's a shapeshifter, always slipping away. But when seized, clasped tight and held continuously in Menelaus's arms ('We held tight with unyielding courage'), Proteus is obliged to resume his original form, an old man of the sea, solemn and wise, who sagely answers the questions he is asked. A story which reminds us that while we may feel the need to take the most varied and contradictory forms in order to attract, rejuvenate, extend or pick up the course of a life, we can become ourselves again when held by firm and obstinate arms that won't let us go. As this chatbot doesn't exist, I had to manage on my own. I texted Anna.

When things aren't going well, ask Panchi to hold you tight in his arms and it will all be okay in the end.

How will it all be okay in the end?

Because we're going into phase three of life, when sex gets put on the back burner.

Oh, give me the antidepressants already.

No! We're saving them for when we're really old.

Well, give me some hope then.

One of my friends sent me some reassuring things about our near future. I'll forward you his message.

(Here's the email from my friend Auguste, an architect:

To start with, you're young and good-looking – at least this is how it was for me, let's be clear that I'm speaking for myself – and it's great, you can pick anyone up and fuck as much as you like, you don't even have to think about it, it's all just normal, natural. That goes on until you're about forty or forty-five, let's say. Then you have the hard years, all that feels far away, right, it's just a matter of personal information – you know you're not so young and you feel that you're not so good-looking, that you're heading downhill, but you don't want to – it's a disaster, you want to fight back, you try to, it sort of works but of course it can't last forever, you feel like you're drowning, bleurgh. And then inevitably, sooner or later, you realise it's 'over', that it's not worth

99

the struggle any more, you're screwed. It can happen at fifty-three or at sixty-seven, it varies, but whether you're like me, a wreck who enjoyed life too much and is done for at fifty-three or fifty-four, or whether you turn out to be a silver fox who fought valiantly but is grey-haired all the same, old all the same, it comes down to the same thing, it's pathetic – it's painful. And then, all of a sudden, when you realise the fight is over, you can breathe again – it's over, woohoo! You realise you don't care. You know this is how you are. Then you take what you can get, with relish, and what you can't get you understand, obviously, you know it's normal, so you're not sad, it doesn't make you depressed. It's like you're liberated. So basically, there you have it: until about forty-five, it was all fun and games, then until fifty-three or fifty-four it was panic, struggle, awareness of the imminent disaster – urgh, no fun – and since then it's all been carefree again. I feel like a benevolent and tranquil Buddha.)

In a perfect illustration of the adage about bad things coming in pairs, the day Adel disappeared Rim got a phone call from her father. Jiji breathlessly announced that he'd just left her mother, who at that moment was sitting on the swing in the garden in Neuilly-sur-Seine with a bottle of sleeping pills in her hand. Well, that wasn't his problem any more, because he'd met a girl who was both nicer and younger, but he was passing on the information. End of conversation. As Rim's younger brother was a bartender in Thailand, my friend had realised straight away that this scene out of a TV movie was destined entirely for her. After hanging up the phone, Rim messaged us to ask if we could come out to the suburbs with her. Out to the chestnut trees and empty avenues. Still reeling from Adel's vanishing act, Anna refused to take the Métro, which I'd never seen her do. She came to pick me up in a taxi: 'What are you doing? Get down here, Armelle, the meter's running, and so is the engine.' So at 9 p.m. our trio found itself in the rust-coloured hallway of my childhood. Before ringing the doorbell, Rim advised us not to resist her mother's charm but on the contrary to give in to it, to make her feel better. She gave us a password, 'firefighter', which we would use to show one another we weren't fooled.

Emmanuelle opened the door wearing a fuchsia silk robe and too much make-up, possibly drunk too. She overplayed the good mood. 'Come in, girls! Who wants sushi?' she asked, huskier than usual.

'Me!' I cried like I was six.

The living-room decor hadn't changed: Louis XV furniture, Chinese vases, little lacquered boxes, dusty rugs. During dinner, Emmanuelle smoked an entire packet of Gitanes Brunes and Anna and I asked her questions about all the celebrities she'd helped travel over the course of her career.

'It's better than being a firefighter!' I said regularly.

An angel of love was passing over the three of us.

Emmanuelle loved Anna, whom she was meeting for the first time and whom she found even more charming than me back when I was in my prime. The evening carried on like this: on the sofa, watching *Nouvelle Star*, the French version of *Pop Idol*. We picked at the sushi and got through two bottles of white wine. In the ad breaks, we made fun of Jiji's rampant male menopause. 'Even under a cold shower he's still too hot,' said Emmanuelle. I was really into the TV programme, but I went to the loo frequently because I was equally fascinated by how my adult size altered the apartment. All the distances were shortened. The volumes, divided. *What is with this tiny little kitchen at the end of this tiny little hallway?* I put my hands on the corners of the walls. I was tempted to lie down on the floor to measure how many of me – at my definitive length – could fit between Rim's old bedroom and her brother's. To sit on the floor and watch Rim's dead cats go past and to hear our childish voices, travelling through the years, first talking admiringly about how beautiful our piano teacher Marina was, then inventing wild sex scenes with her as the star.

After a while, Emmanuelle nodded off and Rim tenderly took her to bed. Once Rim was back in the living room, she said: 'The problem is, tomorrow she'll wake up again.'

9

The Founder's Office

The *Arts* offices were outside Bréguet-Sabin Métro station, near the Place de la Bastille. After two years at the women's magazine in Asnières, Anna and I were both poached within three weeks of each other, in 2010, by this highbrow weekly culture magazine that was in free fall when it came to print sales but was being carried by a new shareholder. At the time, Rim was freelancing and presenting a music show on student radio. Six months after we joined, I gave her name to the editor-in-chief. She was offered a job, which she didn't waste five minutes in accepting.

To prepare Anna for the arrival of my childhood friend, I sent her an email that took two hours to write, in which I went over the longevity of my friendship with Rim. The central message was that we were more like sisters than friends. I was afraid Anna would see herself fading into the background. And I was dreading them meeting. On paper, they had nothing in common. One needed to build up her conceptual intelligence like a tower, while the other used the piano to purge herself of existential concerns. Anna wouldn't buy Rim's professional detachment; she would be irritated by the tailcoats she wore to work, her thick mascara and her way of saying 'do you know what I mean?' when she wanted to talk seriously. Anna's analytic depth, meanwhile, risked passing Rim by entirely; she would find her too much of a know-it-all, too intrusive. Neither of them liked being given orders, though both liked giving them. Their relationship got off to a slow start, but in time something solid developed between them. Six months after my introduction email to Anna, they did something without me for the first time. It was a meeting with Benoît Hamon, in 2011, the year before François Hollande appointed him to the Ministry for the Economy. Watching them leave the office, I wondered if they would discover – by talking about what I had said about one to the other and vice versa – who I really was.

Then, one Sunday when I was on call, walking past Rim's total mess of an office, I saw a pile of books covered in Post-it notes with Anna's handwriting and I realised they were becoming friends. There was a book on forgotten women in history, another about René Dumont, the first ecologist presidential candidate. Politics was something that united them. While I watched the intimate films of Ryūsuke Hamaguchi (whom I consider the Japanese Rohmer) in chronological order, they went on protests together. *Meet at the Place de la République at 2 p.m.*

As for our complicity as a trio, it was consolidated in the FO (pronounced 'eff-oh'). FO for 'founder's office'. In the *Arts* building, at the end of a corridor, this majestic room contained an oval marble table, leather sofas (red, brown and dark green), big velvet curtains and two Paul Klee lithographs. Dated, masonic decor. Since the death of the magazine's founder, the room had been left untouched. We weren't allowed to eat or drink in there, but we could sit and talk. It was in that room, a relic of the golden age of the press, that interstitial space that eluded work, that we were in the habit of meeting up at the end of the day to talk about our Tunisian lovers or our growing climate anxiety. It was also in there that Anna heard my childhood friend play the piano for the first time. While I was listing the recent ill effects of lactose on my stomach, I saw Rim's black leggings cross the room and sit down at the piano. She pulled off the cover with a jerk and put it in a ball at her feet. She lifted the lid and her hands started to play Chopin's Waltz Op. 64 No. 1. A piece that begins with finger movements so rapid it's hard to believe. A virtuosic display you can also play more gently, but which Rim takes as a challenge. A piece that she could already play as a child for her parents' friends, while even though I had the same piano teacher, the famous Marina, and the same number of lessons as her under my belt, I was still wondering which key was middle C. As I was already deeply familiar with her talent, I had the leisure of watching Anna's reaction – she'd never had any piano lessons. Her eyebrows jumped in surprise. Until that moment, she had thought Rim was a big, lazy drifter, an eternal teenage electro fan, so her talent came as an ambush.

That evening, before going to sleep, I watched a video of the same piece played by Daniel Barenboim in St Petersburg in 1997. It was an open-air concert with thousands of attendees. When he attacks the piece at full pelt, the camera is pointed at him, and the funny part is that, behind him, a white-haired violinist reacts exactly like Anna. Eyebrows raised, slight swaying of the head, and an inquisitive look towards the audience: *Am I really hearing this?* After a few seconds, in the FO, Anna went over to the piano and put her hands on Rim's shoulders, as if that wouldn't get in the way of her playing. Rim, who hates being touched, sped up even more, which I hadn't thought possible.

*

Daniel didn't bat an eyelid when I told him I wouldn't get up. He just said, amused: 'Sleep then, and make the most of it. If you'd been born in Brittany, you'd be the mayor of Pleubian and be in a meeting with a trade union by now.' He left the bedroom, and ten minutes later I heard the front door close. He's taken the boys to eat crêpes at his mother's house, or something like that. I put my headphones back on. I search on Apple Music for Chopin's waltz. I can't find Barenboim's version, only the slightly slower one by Maria João Pires. The first notes touch me so deeply, I feel tears warming my nose. To chase away any kind of real emotion, I quickly click on an old compilation album in my library. Elevator music that was once considered cool: *Café Del Mar, Volume 2*.

*

It was also in the FO that, when we were back from Tunisia, we held our confabs about Juliette. She was our new boss, and had joined from a photojournalism magazine. From day one, Juliette treated us as if we were creatures born of her own body. Even though it was snowing, the walls were creaking from the cold, that first day in the office she was in short sleeves. We should have realised she was cold-blooded then, but Anna, Rim and I didn't suspect a thing. On the contrary, our days soon consisted only of trying to please her. In the evenings, in the FO, that was what we would go over. *Was she pleased with us?*

So how did Juliette end up alienating us? In addition to her charm, her short pixie cut, the sensitive age difference of fifteen years which allowed her to dominate us and us to relate to her at the same time, and her superior intelligence, she was an expert manipulator of the Level of Perceived Esteem (LPE). An effective but diabolical managerial tool, the LPE involves dropping employees from the status of Eighth Wonder of the World to that of useless idiot, seemingly at random. Juliette created a world teetering on a seesaw. One day I was the very best, life itself. The next, my desk was methodically skirted around and it was Anna's face that filled the entirety of her pupils (it's horrible, better not to think about it, but in reality our pupils are transparent, not black).

Over the next few months, my relationship with Juliette became complicated. It's ridiculous, but I could have sworn she was descended from a race of birds with piercing eyes.

Hers emitted green laser beams. She saw right through me, she noticed my squirming and my denials, she destroyed my secret projects. An hour before my first evening class on film-making, while I was still keeping quiet about this desire to change paths, Juliette came to beg me to replace someone as head of department. 'You're the only one who's up to it,' she told me, even though I'd been ignored for the previous three months. As she walked away from my desk, she added: 'Forget about films. That's a little girl's dream.'

In the end, it was when Rim did her back in due to stress that the decision was made in the FO to distance ourselves from Juliette. She must have felt it because, from one day to the next, our conversations became a series of failures, before drying up altogether. I remember that, talking to her, everything I said started to sound like an empty Tupperware container falling to the floor. I had the feeling of using partition-words instead of wall-words. Words that seemed to hold together but which were unconnected to each other, hollow, and didn't support any reasoning. I spoke. She was disappointed. Or at least: I thought she was disappointed. It destabilised me. What I was saying became more and more banal in substance and form, if this was even possible. Let me put it like this: when faced with her, I felt like a weak tennis player. The sort who runs all over the place, spins around and only just manages to return the ball. Juliette got bored, tapped her foot, cut short our conversations. While Anna, with her way of always punctuating our conversations with 'that's interesting, go on', naturally raised my game. That's the mark of a friendship like mine and Anna's, by the way – our conversation was greater than the sum of our respective intelligence.

A year after she arrived, Juliette was recruited by a national daily newspaper. We never saw her again.

*

Time to remember my own 'great awakening', the last in the chronological order and, I have to say, not the least ridiculous. Although this is the most difficult of the three 23 May mornings that have passed since our trip to Brittany, I can't help but smile when remembering this story.

10

The Love of Chaos

The day before we left Tunisia, I got talking to a man in front of the hotel aviary. He came up to me to ask what I was looking at 'with such wide eyes'. I replied: 'The birds – at least I'm trying to.' He asked: 'There are birds in here?' before leaning his elbows on the railing and agreeing that yes, there were. In the pocket of his light jacket he had a James Ellroy book whose title I couldn't make out. On that first meeting, I learned that his name was Manuel, that he was married and father to a teenage boy, that he was a sport sociologist, a high-level rugby player, and that he'd come to Djerba for the submission of his friend's thesis on Tunisian football. He was a head taller than me. He had patches of grey hair around his large, sun-reddened ears. A Tic Tac-shaped face. Sort of like a Simpsons character, but in a good way. He dragged his right leg: a sports injury. And he seemed to have a hard-working kind of understanding of the world, which was confirmed by what happened later: Manuel finds it hard to interpret what's happening around him. Everything is initially taken frighteningly literally and it's only later on, like allowing for buffering time, that what he's seen starts to make sense.

The story continued in Paris.

In the beginning, Manuel would look at me like he was hurting somewhere. Every morning at 8.20 a.m., I would receive a straightforward message like: *I like you*. Or: *I'm thinking about your bra*. I had to stop myself writing back *My bra's thinking about you too*, out of fear that he'd take it too seriously: *What's all this about a bra????* When he couldn't reply, he'd just send *Wait*, which I found sexy. I felt like I had control of the situation because I was dazzled neither by the syntax of his messages nor by the sound of his last name. There was nothing mysterious about his psyche, just two main things to bear in mind: that he had affair after affair as a sort of revenge for the fact of being an ugly middle-aged guy; and that his parents' divorce had caused him so much pain that he'd taken divorce off the table for himself. He had an impressive physique, well, the sort whose strength appeals to paranoiacs like me who think the world's going to fall apart tomorrow. Lying in bed, he surpassed me in height and arm span. Basically, it seemed like the perfect kind of adultery – manageable – and Daniel, who was writing a book on the Palaeolithic, didn't suspect a thing. In any case, he took a flexible line on infidelity: 'It can happen, but I don't want to know unless a decision has been made that concerns me.' Manuel and I weren't going to make any decisions of the sort and anyway, after three months of our relationship, my lover made one in the opposite direction: he murmured into my hair that we were going to have to see each other more infrequently because he was changing jobs. I didn't pay attention.

Ten days after his transfer, I was getting far fewer messages from him, and I realised that this distance was changing the way I thought. I no longer sought to rationalise his flaws, even though they were quite major. I started to wait for him to write to me each night, to make myself available at any time and to find it spiritual. I began to believe it was the best sex of my life. Without his texts, which perhaps weren't so badly written after all, it was like my days were flattened. They'd lost a dimension. All that was left was the staff canteen, the Métro and my family. The evening he finally asked me to go with him to the screening of a documentary about class defectors in sport, I hoped our relationship would go back to how it had been before. It was at the Communist Party headquarters in Paris, and the black dress I wore accentuated my red hair. In the lobby, we were waiting for the theatre to open when a renowned sociologist came tottering up to us. Manuel had been her student at university, years earlier. The petite lady had recognised him and, having come on her own, was now counting on clinging to him as if he were a pillar amid a raging fire. They chatted away happily. Weren't far off feeding each other cherry tomatoes. Then, when we were in the theatre, Manuel suggested she sit to his left, knowing full well there was nothing to his right. No chair. Just the aisle. I swallowed my saliva. So he was – consciously

– putting this insurmountable mass of intellectual flesh, this good-humoured sociologist, between us. During the screening, I thought about that and cursed each of the astute observations she made out loud. After the film, the problem was confirmed when Manuel told me outside the Métro: 'I'm not going to have time for us any more.'

'What do you mean?'

'With my new job.'

'What do you mean, with your new job?'

'I may well say a lot of things, you know, but it's still complicated in my head. The most important thing for me is being up to scratch at work.'

'We can see each other less often if you want.'

'I'm not sure. Maybe. But I don't know if I'm going to have time for less often either.'

'I think that if you're not sure, it'd be better if we just called it off.'

'Yes, maybe. I'm sorry.'

I started speaking again: 'All my qualities have tunnelled deep inside my body.'

'Do you have a lot of qualities?'

'Yeah, loads.'

He smiled, then he assured me that it was nothing to do with me: he was at a turning point in his career and he needed to gather all his mental energy to shine in his new role. The violence he was inflicting on me was equal to the change he was going through himself.

'So then, where can I buy this magic power to turn to stone when my interests are threatened?'

'I warned you from the start that I needed to maintain my balance.'

(Is it just me or is there a fundamental difference between men and women here? A gender gap? Is it really because we raise boys in the cult of success and girls in the cult of love? Is sexist education responsible for the prominence of romanticism in the female psyche? Is it because women have been shut up at home for so long that, when they cheat, they do it so wholeheartedly? Or – another hypothesis, which I prefer – is it because, being more independent regarding the maternal figure, and more flirtatious regarding the paternal figure, women develop a higher level of emotional mobility? Desire that's both mobile and determined? Like a robot that bangs into the wall but keeps going anyway. I'm thinking of Freud's patients, the hysterical women of Viennese society. And yes, those women have their descendants who are socially integrated, who change nappies and make breakfast, but who still today, in our more flexible and egalitarian world, feel the constraints of monogamy. Sexual beings, they want to bring down barriers, consume their desires. Consign their middle-class lives and the soulless society around them to napalm. Explode its norms. Actually, these women are in the grand tradition of great men. They want to live a thousand lives, and they have trouble with the idea that organic food and gadgets with Wi-Fi connections could be enough to make them happy. They reject the limitation of sexual experience to conjugal tenderness, and refuse to give up the metamorphosing power of new passion.

Whereas for a man – yes, I'm stereotyping, I'm resorting to generalities, I'm ashamed of myself but I'm going to carry on regardless – desire is more evenly spread out and comfort is prioritised over lots of other things. Love is something that plays out on the outside, like a tennis match. That's how the Duke de Nemours made the decision to give up the Princesse de Clèves, the titular character in Madame de La Fayette's 1678 novel. 'But to give up on this enterprise, which had seemed so difficult and so glorious to him, required another of sufficient grandeur to occupy him. He set his sights on taking Rhodes, which he had already given some thought.')

Rhodes, a new job.

Sorry, I've got a new goal now.

Ah.

Buried in his new responsibilities, Manuel never asked to see me again. I had been wiped from the surface of the earth. I passed him once or twice in the street and he avoided my eyes – he'd rather keep my existence outside of his consciousness. I didn't miss him as a person, but he had opened a narcissistic wound and caused a purely reflexive kind of suffering. *What did I do wrong? What should I have done differently?* I envied him when I thought of Rilke's words, 'To work is to live without dying.' When it comes to work, in contrast to when it comes to love, you can be too generous, giving your whole life without imposing yourself on anybody. After two months of silence, I sent a message.

How are things going? Just about okay?
Just about… Fifteen-hour days… How about you?
Yeah, all good.

And now we have the emotional trap I've been falling into constantly ever since texting was invented.

First stage: I was proud of myself for being so laconic. *Yeah, all good.* Perfect. I said it to everyone around me.

Second stage: an hour later, since he hadn't continued the conversation, I felt guilty for being so laconic. Did he think I was mad at him for breaking up with me? Or that I was sulking?

Third stage: the first rule of texting dictates that you must never, ever double-text. And anyway, I had found his excessive use of ellipses (a third of his message!) ridiculous. But I was becoming convinced I'd wrecked any chance of friendship with my aggressive reply.

Fourth stage: I sent another text.

I sent a photo of the sunny cafe terrace I was sitting on: a pathetic wink to a habit we'd had during our relationship of sending each other pictures taken around Paris. From the photo, you could tell which neighbourhood I was in. Ten minutes later, my phone buzzed. Manuel's reply: *I love Père-Lachaise.* That's all. In a cartoon, my chair would have collapsed under me. What could I reply to that? I decided to leave it there. On that absurd sentence (or one that made a lot of sense, if you thought about how he was burying us). I also started to laugh. I called Anna, who was still at the video calls stage with Adel, and she told me: 'You know, by its nature, an extramarital affair destroys your life or destroys itself. It's exhausting. Let it go.'

That day, when Daniel saw me come home looking all grey, he understood. 'Your body doesn't belong to me, I didn't buy it,' he said. 'But given how grumpy whatever you're going through is making you look, this guy must be a bit of a dick. And we all know where these monkey parades lead. To page 848 of *Belle du Seigneur*, the point when everyone is yawning. So at least think about what you're doing.' I found his remarks condescending, but they also raised a big question. The biggest question of all when it comes to relationships. Should you take the risk of starting all over again (to relive the burning passion of pages three and four) or prioritise the depth of a relationship that's good for you? Can you do both, and do both properly? What kind of life do you want? Can an artistic life push away the desire to stray? What kind of solitude will the freedom you demand eventually crash into? And incidentally, what kind of woman did I want to be? And if the answer is Andie MacDowell, what did she do? According to her Wikipedia page, the actor stayed with the father of her children for thirteen years and since then she's been drifting from man to man with her silvery hair, as beautiful as she was thirty years ago, listing her lovers to a fascinated Hugh Grant: 'Two – hairy back.'

A woman of violent emotions and slow mechanisms (it takes me donkey's years to get to a state where I'm no longer in love), I spent several weeks getting over this empty affair. To help, I read different books about falling out of love. In Pascal Rambert's play *Love's End*, he describes it as the desire to evade the gaze of the other person. Their surveillance. But when the relationship isn't worn out through the everyday, the process of falling out of love takes place over an incompressible and indefinite amount of time. When the process is complete, it feels like the moment when, having swum a long way out and then turned around, the swimmer's feet finally touch the sand. You can't anticipate it precisely, but it always comes in the end. Bam, impact. Of the fantasy, of the sublime, of the mass of water that carried you, nothing remains. Once back on solid ground, the spell is broken and the beloved suddenly appears to you as everyone else has always seen him. Silence and tranquillity settle within you. Silence: as concrete as a chunk of apple in your throat. The questions are all worn out. Now the idea of getting in touch with them doesn't spark your imagination any more. The moments shared with the other person fall back to their market value. You're still soft on their shortcomings, but they no longer form the basis of any cult. They become an ex, i.e. a person we message from time to time, for no real reason, just when an accumulation of fuzzy circumstances triggers, for a second, a swell of nostalgia. In *Jane: A Murder*, the American writer Maggie Nelson investigates the murder of her young aunt, who was a law student at the time. She gets in touch with her relative's old boyfriend who, thirty years after the fact, remembers their love perfectly. His memories are so clear... Reading that passage, I thought: Relationships end, but they stay with us. I understood that an emotional inheritance exists that you can register with the notary. I thought that was worth remembering: after the passion and the pain comes the best moment, when the accounts are closed and what has been lost becomes an asset again. Desire is no longer a nail driven into the stomach. It's conserved like a transplant. It will be conserved for as long as memory holds out. This complicity, this tacit agreement that something unique and sometimes magnificent has happened, is reassuring.

Or at least it was before Brittany.

The evening of 31 December 2014, at the Azur, we celebrated our last night in Tunisia with hummus and kosher wine. We danced to Kendrick Lamar's first album in jeans and swimming costumes and, since the sun was setting in the line of the window and it was bright and red and lit us up like a spotlight, we were ablaze. It was the final scene of this soothing escapade in Tunisia, the peak of our post-maternity teenage rebellion. The disappointments were all still to come. That night, we played Tunisian Monopoly and then some tarot games, and Rim won everything because she had the extreme patience to count the cards. It was one of those special moments in life when nothing negative is in the air. We were all on the same page, laughing about the same things, sharing the same fears. Once my mother told me she was curious to know what the last moments of life would be like. She hoped they would be interesting, even though my grandmother had spent hers throwing the bed-covers on the floor. As for me, I hoped these moments of joy between friends would encircle us until the point of exhaustion. I fell asleep on one of Anna's legs as she was telling me I should take film-making more seriously. Why not make a film about female friendship? 'Get a move on. Otherwise life will pass you by, it'll be like you haven't lived.' Those were the last words I heard.

On the flight back to Paris, I created the WhatsApp group 'The Great Tunisian Awakening', the successor to 'Atlantic Babies', and in the two years that followed thousands of messages flowed down that channel. Lots of advice about our lovers from Djerba. Extracts from books or articles on motherhood or keeping the spark alive in your relationship (Belgian therapist Esther Perel: 'Act as though your partner is going to leave you that very evening, every day'), the usefulness of doing so ('Perhaps we form relationships in order to become the creatures of words that we truly are, to make the speaking-being arrive, as Lacan would put it'), overthinking (a repetitive fixation that feeds the heartache rather than exhausting it) or ageing as a woman (militant feminist Gloria Steinem: 'Between the ages of twelve and sixty, hormones and assigned gender roles stack the deck against us. With old age, our true natures thankfully get the upper hand again. I'm becoming as free again as the little eight-year-old girl who loved climbing trees'). We also exchanged many selfies, each one with a finger held to one side of the nose: the gesture of solidarity Anna had invented, on the spot, when we'd said goodbye at Charles de Gaulle airport after that strange week together.

II
WEST

At 2 p.m., Daniel comes home. Without asking me, he puts a plastic chair out on our balcony, which is still bare and covered in cigarette butts. It's so I'll get up, he says, and so he can air out the bedroom, which 'smells of illness'. I accept, if only so he'll leave me alone again. I put on a jumper over my pyjamas, pull on my thick sports socks and go and sit outside to contemplate the building opposite. On the second storey, the floor is covered by a tarpaulin and one of the inside walls has a hole in the middle. That apartment is in the same state as me.

1

The Chill

What happened next is this. Three and a half years after Djerba, in March 2018, we went to north Brittany. I remember that there was a strong wind blowing through the streets of Paris the morning we left. I did the maths on the Métro and worked out that it must be the thirty-third Gare Montparnasse meet-up of my life. As usual, I was forty minutes early. In the Relay shop, I bought an iPhone charger – it was unbranded but had the right cable. I also messaged the girls to let them know where to find me: by a platform with no train, far away from the departures board, which pointlessly exacerbates the wait. I untangled my headphones and put on the forty-eighth minute of *La traviata*, when Germont, Alfredo's father, explains to Violetta that she must break it off with his son to save their family's honour and she replies: 'Ah, *comprendo*.' It's what I listen to when I'm worrying about something, to remind myself that things could be worse.

Since Tunisia, we had often talked about going on another trip together, and the previous Tuesday, in the Indian restaurant near our office during our first lunch together as a trio in a long time, the idea had come up again. Anna suggested a weekend in Le Havre (because she loved the architect Auguste Perret). We considered the logistics for about ten seconds before it became clear no one was really into it. But a few hours later, I turned it all around. I emailed them a link to an article in *Ouest-France* about an old lightkeeper's cottage available to rent in Morlaix Bay. Seeing the spectacular photos of the little island, discussions started up again. It would be something original. A good story to tell. It would allow us an 'immediate rapport with the sea', as Anna put it, quoting Foucault. We would try to recreate our Tunisian harmony, even if everything was different now, I thought. Leaving work that evening, we agreed to make a reservation for the following week. When Anna got home, she gave her daughter a bath and then took care of booking the train tickets and three kayaks to reach the island, and I thanked her a hundred times over text. That same evening, my younger son interrupted me while I was reading to him: 'Do that again so I can count the lines.' 'Do what again?' 'Frown.'

It was a brilliant idea to get away from it all for a few days. But seeing Rim and Anna converging on me in Gare Montparnasse, my chest puffed up like an amphibian's neck. I felt like I was carrying the weight of this trip, and indeed of our relationship in general, on my shoulders. I sensed danger. I asked myself if it was smart to isolate ourselves on a desert island when our friendship was going through such a difficult time. Before, our conversations

had been fluid, with equal contributions and virtuous disagreements – we wound each other up for a laugh. But over
the last few months, we'd wandered little by little into an
era of permanent contradiction. The cutting remarks were
non-stop. When I thought about what our main response to
each other had become, it was an English word that came
to mind: *belittling*. And when, in the best-case scenarios,
what we had to confide didn't immediately provoke nega-
tivity from the other two, it was simply cut down instead:
*Look, what you've just said reminds me of this funny thing
to do with me.*

Our trio didn't work any more. Youth, sisterhood,
pregnancy and early motherhood were all behind us; now
each of us was preoccupied with the approach of middle
age. At thirty-eight, we were all engaged in the notorious
search for meaning that comes with the second part of
life. No longer any time for debriefs over text and things
like that. Rim was constantly practising the piano, with
the secret goal of playing a piece written by her great-
grandfather with a crazy pedalling technique. She would
work at her sheet music all night instead of going out and,
in front of the coffee machine the next morning, would tap
the dark circles under her eyes and declare: 'I see everyone
else out having fun on Instagram but it does nothing for me,
it all seems so empty.' Anna had started a course of didactic
psychoanalysis, three times a week, which distanced her
from us and which I regarded with some jealousy because I
wasn't as invested in my own cure. She talked about psycho-
genealogy so much that sometimes I saw she was disgusted

with herself (given how much less time she spent discussing, say, the problem of climate change).

As for me, for the past year I'd been renting an old nun's cell in the Goutte d'Or neighbourhood, where I churned out short film screenplays at an industrial rate. Most of them were lying dormant in a drawer, but I had succeeded in getting the latest one produced and it had had some success at festivals. To get to my desk, which quickly became my second home, I first had to pass through the dead skins of the butchers' shops on Rue Myrha, the organic counterparts of the fabrics in the Saint-Pierre market the other side of Boulevard Barbès. The day I got the keys, Daniel gave me silver sponges, a mini hoover and a purple toilet brush as a present. He said to me, 'I'll look after the kids, you get to work.' Then he left me there, in that high-ceilinged box with vines tumbling around the window frame, perfectly alone, and I had a divine revelation. I rediscovered the natural state of my childhood, a profound solitude which gave me the sensation of rocking my head backwards and forwards. I realised the extent to which other people burdened me with their very existence, and I admit that my thoughts turned to how quickly I might cut people off, so much did this asceticism suit me.

When it came to love affairs, we had temporarily given them up. Now getting on for forty, we had gone back to the fleur-de-lys-patterned corridor with a kind of relief. The concept of bikinis and toned arms was gently drifting away. Those *fizzing* feelings, the urges, the hyper-existence: all that would be waiting in the next life. We looked upon the fathers of our children with indulgence and resignation. On the day we set off, all three of us were wearing Saint James sailor jumpers, white with blue stripes, but that was where the harmony ended. Rim and Anna no longer profited from the considerable benefit of the doubt that I now granted only to my children and my own opinions. On the platform, I watched their backs as they walked ahead of me and weighed up what they brought to my life. I was tightly wound. I felt like one sapped my energy and the other hadn't stopped bossing me around since we were five years old. And furthermore, I could feel that neither of them had faith in my new professional ambitions. With good reason? Maybe.

Sitting on my seat, I checked without looking that the lid of the grey metal bin next to my leg was attached to its base (it was, for once) and thought about all the questions raised by the first feature-length script I was writing. On the back of my closed eyelids, between a red line and some green spots, appeared my childhood resolution, to be *neither a victim, desecrated on the ground, nor a tormentor who only listens to the sound of their own voice*. A balance all the more difficult to strike now that writing was making me be both at the same time. It fused the weak and the strong in me. It consolidated my subjectivity, to the detriment of others. I was ceasing to be the perpetually dominated one, becoming a master of narrative instead, and so on. 'Description is a means of vengeance,' wrote Flaubert to Sand. So, seeing them put their bags up on the overhead shelf, above the table seats, I asked myself: Is it possible to exploit your joint memories and keep your friends? To still be loved when you've changed your main objectives in life? And the pleasure of listening only to your own voice, your own idea of things, your patchy memory alone – is it possible to feel that without destroying everything around you?

The train had reached full speed. There was a clear morning light, every detail of the landscape could be seen, and I was playing my little game of sympathising with homeowners who'd had the TGV line land at the bottom of their gardens in the nineties: *nice stone farmhouse, bad luck*. Slouched in their seats, my friends were both looking at their phones when, at Guingamp, a couple boarded the train and sat on the pair of seats across the aisle from us. I put them at about twenty. The boy had a delicate face grafted onto a thick Javier Bardem-esque neck. With her prominent chin, the blonde girl had a half-moon profile. Underneath her raincoat she was wearing a floaty blouse from another century. Pretty, cold, her mouth barely opened when she spoke. No efforts made at diction, her manner that of an annoyed princess, her speech a tapestry of cutting remarks. 'I only realised how stupid your brother is when we were at the cafe,' we heard her say. They were adults who had yet to put down roots in real life. Anna and I closed our eyes to eavesdrop better.

From what I understood, Clémence was starting a law course at the University of Oxford, where Louis already studied. To battle the feeling of insignificance, of professional irrelevance, which had seized me, I started a new WhatsApp group called 'Critical analysis of passengers

72 and 73'. Anna came online straight away, whereas Rim waited fourteen vibrations. Her attention was finally caught thanks to the insistence of the notifications generated by Californian servers, even though her arm was brushing against mine. She leaned forward abruptly to see who we were talking about, looked at them while pulling on the straw of her kiwi smoothie and rolled her eyes to the heavens. *Top students, they breathe boredom*, she wrote in the group. She asked if we found them attractive. I admitted that yes, I did – the boy's neck, but also the girl, who would definitely be able to run naked without losing her dignity. On the attractiveness of the couple Anna didn't respond; she's one of those rare people who dare to evade questions asked over text. But all her senses were straining towards the couple, and it was clear she was as fascinated as I by their aristocratic aura. None of the three of us had grown up with the combo that makes you invincible: emotional security, inherited self-importance and financial power. Five minutes later, in the group:

Anna: *Louis de Lampierre and Clémence d'Astor.*

Me: *What?*

Anna: *Our neighbours' names.*

Me: *Sounds like a joke.*

She didn't reply, so I added: *Hey look, the guy's family tree goes back to 1196 + a bust of one of his ancestors is sitting in the Galerie des Batailles in the Palace of Versailles.*

Anna: *GHA* ['good heavens above', her favourite expression]. *A Lampierre has achieved some great feat in every century.*

Me: *But in our century, all Louis has done is throw a pencil at the girl.*

Anna: *Sure, but how are you supposed to be heroic on a train?*

Me: *By climbing on the roof? Distributing provisions?*

Anna: *His great-grandfather won several decisive battles in the First World War.*

Rim: *All our great-grandfathers did that.*

Me: *Yeah, but ours weren't commanding squadrons.*

Anna: *Ours fell in the mud.*

Rim: *Speak for yourselves. We had medals in my family.*

As we pulled into Morlaix, Louis and Clémence also got up, and we all walked single file towards the doors. Before the train stopped, and driven by a childish urge, I took my book out of the front pocket of my suitcase and said loudly: 'Now we're on holiday, I'm going to finish *The Magic Mountain* this weekend. It will have taken me four days, this book.' Louis looked at me: Thomas Mann still has an effect. Anna winked at me, the first time in centuries.

Walking through the station, I considered continuing to talk about Mann, but it would have been pathetic, too obvious what I was up to. The couple peeled off to the right, towards a vintage American car parked across the forecourt, from which a fifty-something woman with a sunburned chest appeared. With no trace of irony, the young man cried out, 'Hello, Virginie!' Clémence's mother. The chin, identical to her daughter's, must have persisted through the centuries. She was wearing a pink T-shirt with the words ST CLOUD PARISH. The three aristocrats got in the convertible. Our suitcases at our feet, hands by our sides, Anna and I watched it wriggle out of the car park while Rim played with a lighter. It should be known that my friend never reveals any fascination with other people. She defends herself from their successes with bursts of ego that make her believe she too can do anything. She arms herself, barricades herself, so as not to let other people's achievements get to her. And that way she creates a haziness around the true position she occupies in the world. Which is undoubtedly an asset, but it is irritating. As Victor Hugo once put it, and as I've repeated to her often since I learned it, 'In admiration, there is a certain strengthening quality that dignifies and grows understanding.'

Our little group silently went over to the taxi rank, where a young woman with a cone-shaped piercing in her chin opened her car's back door for us. 'Hi, I'm Anne-Gaëlle. But everyone calls me Anne-Ga. Get in!' Anna asked if she could sit next to her, in the front. The girl nodded, and as if that gesture now gave her carte blanche to take control of the whole vehicle, my friend also opened the windows and turned down the radio. France Bleu defeated, she appointed herself boss of the car. I knew what came next: she would steer the conversation, dive into the girl's life to get all the details. To slow down her inevitable transformation into a 'basic Parisian', Anna likes to question anyone from elsewhere in France on their financial situations. She takes other budgets than her own into consideration. I heard our driver explain to her that she parked in Morlaix because the Brest harbour was empty these days. It made for a long drive each day, yes. Anna egged her on with an 'it must cost you a lot in fuel' and the girl hurried to give her an amount. Anna followed up by asking about her monthly income. 'It doesn't pay much,' Anne-Ga admitted; she was only left with six hundred euros to live on. 'But driving back and forth across Brittany, it's not bad, you know. It could be worse.' (Only when I heard her say that she lived in Landerneau did I pipe up from the back seat: 'Ah! Like in the saying "That's going to make noise in Landerneau".' It's a classic French saying, meaning word is going to get around fast. But – how was this possible? – it didn't mean anything to her. The social media generation? An alien? Or perhaps, without realising, I'd spoken with a weird Belgian accent.) After having gone over the cost of rent and of fish, Anna started to lose interest. She closed her window, put the radio back on and told the girl that the area would still be inhabitable in twenty years, when it'd be two degrees warmer.

The old black radio set, with no USB port, was showing midday. No one was talking any more as we drove slowly along the Morlaix river. At low tide, carpeted with seaweed, its bed looked like a path from a fairy tale. Further away, the Carantec commune looked out of place compared to the rest of north Brittany. It was a rich, clean, well-built, verdant seaside resort. The kind of place which didn't inspire any particularly strong sentiments. Nothing like the town of Tréguier, for example, less than a hundred kilometres away, with its low skies, its beams, its cathedral, its medieval hills, its thousand-year-old artichoke fields and, when it finally appears, its sea that bears all the weight of the past. On the coast, at Plougrescant, sepia ghosts have even been known to lift their heads from the water to give you an enigmatic smile. At Carantec, though, the water looked new. Limpid and full of coral. Turquoise near the shore because of the shallow depth of the bay; dark and covered with little patches of light further out. A Caribbean sea, punctuated by small granite islands. Through the dirty windscreen, Anne-Ga pointed out the Chateau du Taureau, painted gold by the midday sun. A fort in the Boyard style, built after a raid by the English in 1522 (followed by the massacre of those same drunken soldiers by the French, she said, and I remarked that I was pleased to hear it). Slowing down to give us time to admire it, Anne-Ga murmured: 'Once you're on the island, you can't get tired of looking at the Taureau. It's close and far away at the same time.'

Next to the fort was the Île Noire, a rock which had inspired Hergé while he was staying a few kilometres from there. In Locquénolé, Anne-Ga added. Seeing the girl pointing out these tourist sites, I thought of Daniel who, while he's driving, points with his finger at the road he's on to remind himself to follow it. I would have preferred to spend the weekend with him; it would be less of an effort. Anna's fair hair was flattened on the headrest in front of me. Anne-Ga was showing her the island we were going to: 'You'll be spending your next two days down there.' About the size of two football pitches, its only buildings were a lighthouse and an adjoining cottage. The lighthouse had been built in 1857 to reduce the number of shipwrecks in the bay and, thanks to it, the bodies had indeed stopped piling up on the sea floor, said Anne-Ga. For over a hundred years, lightkeepers had lived there in succession, until it was automated in the sixties. During the half-century that followed, the island had stayed as empty as a drowned village. In 2008, the year they'd been able to install electricity, it had opened as a holiday home: so for ten years tourists had been disturbing its silence every weekend. Except in the case of storms.

'The tourists are very careful. There have been no accidents to report,' said our driver as she turned abruptly onto a road leading up to the seafront. Two minutes later, she pulled up by a beach strewn with catamarans. 'The manager of the boat centre should be waiting for you.' We got out, made gestures of thanks at her, and, strangely, she drove off without saying goodbye.

2

Kill Instagram

As the sea was choppy, the manager of the boat centre decided to take us to the island in a dinghy rather than trust us with the kayaks we'd booked for the journey. He was a tall man, and he wore an apple-green life jacket, even on dry land (even to print out the bill). 'His Breton pallor has been ruined by that heatwave in February,' Anna said worriedly to me. It was stressful how she went on about the climate non-stop. But it had to be said: the guy's skin was indeed a radiant, even brown. And seeing him, a few minutes later, pushing his orange boat along the yellow sand, gave me the impression of being in a technicolour world. This Fauvist period Willem Dafoe made us sit on the same side of the boat, which was counter-intuitive, and didn't steer towards the island in a straight line, which was even more so. He was clearly following some maritime route only he knew.

Resting on the boat's steering wheel, the manager's hand was as large as a spade. The palm was taut and dried out by the salt. *Louët*, he told us, means 'grey' in Breton. Like the colour of his eyes, which are *doualagad*, I thought. Anna demanded other colours. He shouted words to her over the noise of the motor. *Mouk* meant purple, red was *ruz*, and *damruz* (almost red) translated as pink. This banter made him speed up without realising it. Anna's lips formed the word *mouk*, which she found funny, over and over. The boat was going too fast, and I was afraid of falling off backwards and being decapitated by the propellers. Anna's fair hair flapped against her oversized parka. Her natural habitat is at the top of a mountain or outside buildings with distinctive architecture, but she was also very beautiful right there, out at sea.

As we approached the landing stage, Rim got out her phone. Fauvist Dafoe had cut the motor; the boat was pitching. She waited for the island and the sea to fill the frame in the ideal two-thirds:one-third ratio, snapped away at the landscape, applied filters, and in less than a minute had posted several pictures to Instagram, then added them to her story along with a Nolwenn Leroy remix. On her impressively well-followed page, Rim posted pictures of concerts, the dried flowers Niels hung from the ceiling, all kinds of neon lights, contemporary artworks arranged in cold churches, and videos of her playing the piano barelegged. Over her head, on the boat, a subliminal look passed between Anna and me: we have historically thought badly of Instagram. We think that on one side there are the people who treat it like masturbation, and on the other, voyeurs trying to get some perspective on the pleasure they're exposed to. At the time, Anna liked to sleep in a T-shirt that read KILL INSTAGRAM and hated the feeling of FOMO the platform fed in her, reducing her own life to a mini life in comparison to other people's supposedly fascinating ones. 'I don't understand why people agree to making adverts out of their own existence, to contributing to this oppressive propaganda, when they know full well they're fighting with all they've got, like everyone else, and behind all the pictures of beach paradises there are problems like clogged toilets and coke addictions,' she would say when it started to bother her again. Then she'd dive into psychoanalytic considerations. She'd describe the infantile narcissism which lets a grandiose, exhibitionist and all-powerful Ego take charge. It was already hard enough to give in to adulthood without having to put up with all these manipulated images too, she said. In private, Rim agreed that Anna was a discontented empress, frustrated that Instagram showed her all these unattainable territories. And also that, being a theatre critic, she wasn't exactly modern. As for me, I used the platform in full awareness. I didn't shy away from the regressive pleasure of 'likes'. When I posted a picture, I visualised myself doing great jetés in a pink tutu. Happiness and sharing are one and the same, I thought to justify myself. The beauty of a landscape feels hollow if there's no one there to see it with you. But I never posted selfies, because even though I understood the thrill that comes from showing off your best side to a thousand watching eyes, I always failed to find a pretext to do so. I've noticed that recently the way people do it is to couple them with some context, like in a comic strip frame ('first day of autumn'). Mostly, the fact that people caption their own faces with metadata depresses me, but I can also find it deeply moving some-times, seeing these unsolicited proof-of-life photos, these self-portraits that reinforce an idealised self. I'm touched by these artisanal photo shoots, for what they say about the difficulty that – rightly – exists, of not always resembling these images.

The boat was pitching so much that Willem Dafoe gave up on us disembarking on our own. The sailor grabbed the concrete platform with both hands and held on so tight all his fingers turned white. He brought the dinghy up to the slab using the strength of his thighs and hooked the rope tucked under his arm onto the mooring bracket. The bulg-ing edges of the inflatable boat banged against the rocks. Willem hesitated; clearly he'd judged us as not being sporty, unfair on Rim and her muscly shoulders. My childhood friend went first; she put her hands on the platform and hoisted up her body with the strength of her arms alone. An industrial goods lift in another life. Willem whistled in admiration, handing up her big Adidas bag. Then – pres-sure – it was my turn. Rim held out her hand to me like on the day we'd climbed the statue of the Duke of Orléans. For a second I thought of my busted elbow, the feeling of rustiness, of heavy mechanics, that goes back to that day, and though she was sweetly offering to help me join her, and though I was looking up at her, I loved her less.

That extended hand reminded me of the duke, but also of our mornings spent at the swimming pool in Vanves. I couldn't get out without the ladder, and Rim would pull me from the water. Those hours in the pool were unpleasant because my friend spent her time doing double backflips from the highest diving board, the ten-metre one, while underneath my mother swam against the softening of her body. Above, I had what I would never be, and below, what I would become. Out of the unchlorinated Vanves water, Rim walked slowly towards me with her towel around her neck. Once she was alongside me, she said: 'If I couldn't do sport, I'd die.' Impossible to verify. But I was struck by her romanticism. Stop showing off, I thought. We're all going to die one day, however much sport we do. I was so exasperated by her cheery tone that I retreated to my domain: the slides. Then, shortly before midday, I cracked. Drawn in by her popularity among the other children, the accumulation of fans around her, I went to join her on the ten-metre board, just to show all those bumpkins who her real friend was. Once I was up there, it was impossible to turn back, and the general consensus was that it was my turn to jump. By some unknown physical or mental process, my terrified body fell from the platform as if someone had pushed it. Torso forwards, one leg sticking out. On impact, my thigh hit the water straight on, and my adductor muscle tore from top to bottom like a TV dropped on the floor. Stinging, feeling like all the little bones in my leg had been shuffled into new places, but feigning nonchalance, I got out of the pool. Sitting on a metal bench, wrapped in a too-small towel (from the armpits to the hips), I felt like a trussed-up tenderloin fighting to survive in the world of humans. A strawberry jelly stuck in a rubber glove. It was the fishing-net dress and the self-hatred all over again.

And that was just the start. The worst came later, in the car, when Rim made me believe that I'd lost my wits because of the fall. Her post-swim fun. You have to understand that as a child I imagined my brain as a pipe, always at risk of a thought that was too huge, or too complex, blocking it like a sink drain. I was scared of suddenly no longer being able to read or speak. Rim, who knew this, started up an inconsequential conversation, then ended by saying in her husky voice: 'Well there it is, no doubt about it, you've turned into an idiot. That's why you shouldn't land on your head.'

'I landed on my leg,' I said, without being certain of it any more. Rim was tackling the underside of her black hair with her plastic hairbrush. With her face covered like that, it was impossible to tell if she was making fun of me. So I set about thinking, to see if I still could. If what she said was true, I thought, I'd have to live without any particular outlook on life. Without aphorisms, paradox, irony, post-irony, metaphysical reflection, which at least gave the impression of expanding the bars of the cage. If you lose neurons, it's very slowly, I reassured myself.

My mother was driving in fits and starts. So she didn't have to make us anything to eat, she stopped at the McDonald's near Porte de Champerret on the way back, and since Rim's parents forbade junk food, she added: 'It'll be our secret, girls.' After having wolfed down two meals each (a Happy Meal and a Big Mac), Rim and I, heavy and silent, pushed open the door of her corridor in Neuilly. And then I got my revenge for the morning. Right in front of Emmanuelle, I handed her the McDonald's toy she'd deliberately left on the back seat of the car. 'Here you go, Rim,' I said. 'You forgot this.'

Thanks to Rim's extended hand, I managed to get up onto the platform by walking vertically up the wall. Between that and the guilt for having dropped her in it over the McDonald's, I loved her again. Side by side, Rim and I watched the boat rock more and more. We pulled on the rope to try and stabilise it. Would Anna be able to get out, or would she have to go back with Willem Dafoe, marry him and become a mermaid? She gave it a go several times, couldn't get out on her own, so the sailor went up to her and asked if he could help. She nodded. He grabbed her by the waist, counted to three and lifted her up like a trophy. Then he gave her a little twisting thrust in the air that let her make a dynamic half-turn on herself and land sitting on the concrete. My friend got up elegantly, breaking down each movement. I was fascinated: it was like watching the golden age of figure skating on TV. Once Anna was on her feet, she turned to Willem, who was still watching her, taken with her and amused to be. She waved to him and cried 'Mouk', as if it meant goodbye. He laughed, turned his boat away from her, from us, and didn't wave except for once, his back still turned, at full speed. I winked at Anna: *That's the classic Breton reserve for you. But he's in love.*

The boat disappeared, taking the romcom atmosphere with it. There we were, standing on a concrete slab, at the foot of Île Louët. With Saint James jumpers and no means of transport. The first thing that sprang to mind for me was to check the strength of the phone signal in case a medical emergency befell us. My screen was showing a single bar, and an uncertain one at that. We'd better hope nothing bad happens, I thought, making a mental note to avoid the edges of the cliffs and steer clear of the big black electricity cable that snaked past not far from us. Emerging from the sea, the thick, sinuous cable seemed like an enormous intestinal beast which had fallen asleep on the rocks in the middle of a long journey.

Walking along, Rim took more Instagrammable photos of the rocks, the sea and the sky. She was singing France Gall again; for more than thirty years she'd been imposing on me that smoky voice she thought was so great. Anna was waiting for us twenty steps up, in front of a little pavilion built into the rock. It was a bathroom with an electric-blue floor, and so lovely that we had to be dragged away to go and see the rest. A bit further up, the lightkeeper's cottage looked like a schoolchild's drawing: four windows framed with rectangular stones. I was the only one of us who was Breton and, although I didn't dare say it, out of embarrassment at how I'm always mentally constructing my own immortality, I felt a deep affinity for the place. This place, Brittany, its air and its earth, had shaped me over the generations. *It's here that I'll continue to exist after my life is over, in a way.* I wanted to pull a sword out of the stone here and shout my family name. We fight our transitory nature the best we can, I thought as I lifted the flowerpot the keys were hidden under. I unlocked and pushed open the old wooden door to the house. I let Rim and Anna go in first. There were walls everywhere, the way I like it. This place, cut off from the rest of the world, had escaped the all-encompassing craze for I-beams.

To our right the kitchen opened out, with gas canisters on the floor and drawings of seabirds on the walls. But what caught the eye immediately was a spiral of adhesive tape that curled down to the floor. Sellotape, my deepest fear. The flytrap gave the room a feeling of suffering. Some of the flies were still moving, struggling, and would have almost been able to escape, the tape was so old. This swarming atmosphere reminded me of that awful Damien Hirst work (flies consuming a cow carcass) which had made the front page of our magazine. To the left of the entryway was a dim room with a single window in the shape of a giant ice pop, and two basic metal beds. (If a lightkeeperess had given birth to twins in 1903, they would have slept there before killing each other.) Upstairs, there were two magnificent bedrooms opposite one another, with parquet floors. One was called the Yellow Room because all the furniture – desk, bed, chairs – was yellow, as was the moss on the windowsill. Above the bed, a yellow porthole looked out to sea, while opposite, in the Blue Room, a blue porthole gave a view of the lighthouse studded with lichen, its colour somewhere between grey and white. When you opened the blue door, it made a noise like a man trying to croak out his last words: *Aaaaaoooooh*. I asked to take the Yellow Room because of this scary noise; Anna and Rim agreed and decided straight away to share the Blue Room. Seeing them so happy with the way it had panned out made me regret

145

not thinking it through a bit more, until a minute later Rim threw herself onto the bed along with her bag, messing up the covers, the springs, the very structure of the bed. She'd turned the whole room into a pigsty within two minutes and my doubts had evaporated. Subconsciously, she must have been celebrating our night-time divorce because she knows all too well that, when I'm falling asleep, my left foot goes dead on top of my right, which rubs against the mattress as if it's urgently trying to get to the air. My feet are in a toxic relationship. 'It's masturbation!' Rim used to cry when we were teenagers and we slept top to tail. 'Go and do that somewhere else, Armelle. Get out. The living room, the hall, wherever you want, but not right next to my ear, for fuck's sake.' Twenty years later, she was about to discover that Anna falls asleep like a French king in his cathedral tomb, immobile, her face turned to the ceiling, hands joined on her stomach, and it's impossible to tell, the whole night, whether she's asleep or working out an equation. As for the little bedroom downstairs, the room of the dead twins from 1903, it would stay empty. We had understood it wasn't going to be easy to fall asleep, to give in to psychological retreat and the forgetting of the self, while surrounded by an unthinking liquid. Encircled by a mass of water whose movements are decided by the moon. Out here, the sea was to be feared.

After making her and Rim's bed meticulously, with the bedspread folded neatly on the duvet, which she'd tucked under the mattress on either side, Anna offered to take care of our evening meal. Heading down, our footsteps on the wooden stairs made a racket that must have taken the house itself by surprise. Rim went outside to try to call her daughter, while Anna pushed aside the hundreds of bottles of olive oil left on the worktop by previous inhabitants. Before getting started on the tapenade crostini, she put away all the groceries we'd bought on the mainland and, as she opened and closed the fridge for every single item she put in there instead of leaving the damn thing open, I was struck by a horrible feeling of wasted time. It happened to me a lot in those days. It was oppressive. I realised that I was neither doing nor learning anything worthwhile, even though a year can still be decisive at our age, and I could no longer bear unproductive time. I wanted to get back all those childhood hours spent on Rim's Game Gear, always losing, and those spent admiring myself in the mirror as a teenager. I began to hate small talk. I'd have given anything to be a young man in a Hasidic community studying the Talmud all day. Or to learn a rare language from morning to night. As it was, I had the feeling I was merely hanging around, missing out on some essential thing that would allow me to consider death more calmly. Missing a comment, a method of approach, that would give me a better perspective on it (like this Mallarmé verse, which soothed me for many weeks: 'a shallow stream that's slandered and named Death'). Watching Anna open the fridge again and again, the image of a little round glass from a canteen with the number *83* inscribed on the bottom passed through my head. Eighty-three years, is that it? My knees knocked together and I hung on mentally to what the tarot reader I met in a restaurant as a teenager had said to me: 'You will be so old when you die that dying will be a pleasure.' I had the feeling of floating in the room, and I walked out backwards.

As I went back up to my bedroom, I felt the others' disapproval following me closely. *A girls' weekend, and look at that, she's going off on her own already. Typical Armelle, never a team player.* Sitting on my yellow bed, I could make out their muffled voices through the parquet and thought that they would equally be able to hear the sound of my laptop if I turned it on. I'd brought a paper copy of my screenplay, in case my room didn't have any plug sockets, and I took it out of its folder, but I didn't feel like that either: I was just above their heads, they could come up at any time, and this project was partly about them. So I decided to go and wash, which is always a good interim solution. The bathroom is a refuge: thanks to the patriarchal expectation that women always be fresh as a daisy, no one begrudges them spending time in there. In my Paris apartment, for the lack of having a room of my own, a room that my soul can inhabit, I lock myself in the bathroom for a bit of peace and quiet. I sit on the floor and wait to get sick of it. On Louët, walking back past the kitchen, I announced that I was going to go and look at the nice little pavilion by the water's edge. They didn't reply.

I walked down quickly and, when I pushed open the flaking door, I was dazzled. The thousand tiny panes of a stained-glass window bigger than I was let the whole sky and its reflection in the sea enter the room. All the light bounced off the white walls, the shower curtain, the ceramics, the tiling. I was entering a luminous world. A glass box. I felt moved as I undressed. In the shower, I took off my bra, my pants and my socks. I threw them outside. I turned on the tap; the water was ice-cold. I put a foot, a knee, my head for half a second under the low-pressure flow. I sucked in my stomach so the water wouldn't touch it yet. I pulled back the curtain, still dry and sharp-edged, to bring some yellow into the blue sparkle of the steam. I held my breath, turned up the pressure as far as it would go and put my whole body under the salt water. My skin was laminated and the sea gently lifted the room. I felt it press against my feet. Then, when the sun left the window, I shivered all of a sudden. My skin became rough, my hands turned red and I noticed the ten or so spiders squatting around my feet in the shower tray. I took a towel from a hook and rubbed myself hard, as if I'd escaped a shipwreck. I put my sailor's jumper back on, slid into my jeans and sat on the edge of the huge window. For twenty minutes, I watched the light dancing over the walls. Just before I reached the house again, I thought that I was self-sufficient with a melancholy streak. Individualistic, self-serving, ambitious. A bad friend, these days.

3

The Target Changes Too Quickly

In the kitchen, I found the atmosphere unbearable. My dissidence had unified them in a sort of quasi-honeymoon. Like birds at the start of springtime with their private, synchronised movements. When Anna spoke, Rim laughed for no reason. I could sense that they both had questions about the shower and its practicality, but they were both too annoyed with me to ask them. The word 'selfish' was snapping at my heels. Then finally: 'We waited for you to go and explore the island. But it's too late now it's dark,' Rim said in a dry tone.

Silence. I didn't want to explain myself, pour out everything about the Hasidic schools and the emptiness I felt when I wasn't working. To feel the tears well up in my eyes as they always do when I have to justify myself, even over a tiny thing. I shrugged. I replied that I thought three days would be long enough to explore an island the size of the Place de la Bourse in Paris. To regain some brownie points, I grabbed a pile of plates and took them out onto the patio. Rim put a bottle of wine and some glasses on the table.

Anna arrived with her platter of crostini and an old oil lamp that she set at our feet.

'That's nice, where did you find it?' I asked.

'Next to the bin.'

The evening started off well. Black waves rolled towards the open sea as we discussed our mothers-in-law, one subject that still worked for us. We all revered Panchi's mother because she was Argentine, divorced, took karate lessons and wrote essays about solitude. Daniel's mother is a renowned academic who, even though I have a master's degree, considers me uneducated. 'But your friend has a good understanding of situations,' she often says to Daniel, thinking it's a compliment. It had become an in-joke between the three of us. ('You with the good understanding of situations, do you know where the detergent is?') Niels's fascinated us because of the overdose of misfortune that she'd gone through in one lifetime. Her parents were part of the small group of 759 Norwegian Jews deported from the country between 1940 and 1945. As slender as a young maple tree, the little orphan had been subject to one catastrophe per year ever since. 'Catastrophe' in the etymological sense. That evening, Rim told us about the latest one: a fragment of meteorite had fallen into her garden. The outdoor furniture had been pulverised; no trace of the parasol could be found.

At 9 p.m., the lighthouse lit up and everything changed. A white light swept over our heads with an unbearable regularity. With one arm across her stomach, the other resting on it at a right angle, her glass of red wine held up by her ear, Rim yawned several times in a row. For those who know her well, it's a signal. A signal that has always indicated either the start of a rambling description (an apartment she might have visited, for example, whose lay-out she'd describe, saying, 'And to the right of that room, you've got the hallway,' while of course from the beginning no mental effort at all has been made to follow her and it is therefore impossible to know how far in she is and when it will be over) or a huge burst of self-confidence. I realised it was the latter when she told us she'd found a film utterly terrible to the point of laughing nervously now she was thinking about it again. 'Not poetic,' she said with her husky radio-presenter voice and her hair falling in her eyes. 'Not profound.' She lamented the director's 'delays', his 'indecision'. She lit a cigarette. Anna and I hadn't seen the film, but Rim's opining got on our nerves beyond what was reasonable. Our faces tightened. We were thinking the same thing, namely that non-professionals should always bear their own subjectivity in mind and that certain words should be banned ('profound', 'powerful', 'enthralling'; they're no more than the word 'good' amplified, words used to get yourself noticed). Anna and I also thought that Rim made too few real efforts in life to grant herself the right to destroy other people's work. 'With a film like that, the director insults his own intelligence,' Rim carried on. A sip of wine for Anna, ringing in my ears. Given that I was just starting out in film-making, I took more precautions when it came to criticism. In fact, when negative judgement is made to back up that person's own resistance to change, when it comes from someone who hasn't made equivalent or better efforts in their own life, a critic who, instead of starting by appreciating the initiative, makes a list of everything they personally thought was missing or what they would have done instead, basically when judgement is solely destructive, jealous, self-centred – it makes my blood boil. I thought: Every time you violently critique something, you should ask yourself what you're avoiding doing yourself. But I said: 'Hmm, I'll give that one a miss then.'

'Did Niels hate it too?' Anna asked.

'I went with Zoé,' Rim replied in a tone intended to end the conversation.

Yikes – this was going to be a showdown. I was already exhausted by what was surely coming. For context, you have to know that Zoé, a former journalist who now works in fashion, was Anna's friend and housemate centuries ago, before they fell out over something to do with a copied key. The fight got so out of hand that the lease was terminated and numbers scribbled out of phone books (these days, they'd have blocked each other). Six months before Louët, Rim had met Zoé at the gym in Jaurès. To begin with, I'd gone with her, but the Afrovibe dance workouts tired me out so much I felt like my spine had been turned into a railway track, and I'd cancelled my membership. One evening, Rim was approached by a supple girl, always top of the class. 'You're not a journalist, by any chance?' Three weeks later, Rim and Zoé were sharing a joint membership and getting changed together. Anna couldn't stand that someone she loved also loved Zoé, because that put her version of events (namely that the other girl was out of her mind) in peril, while Rim hated hearing Anna talk about Zoé because her own mind was made up.

In a serious voice, Anna said: 'Apparently she's launched a very tacky clothing brand.'

'I wouldn't put it like that,' Rim replied.

'Oh really? Then why have I only heard bad things about it?'

'You should go and see for yourself, there's a shop near Place de la Bastille. That girl is astonishing.'

'You're the only one to say "astonishing" and not mad.'

'We're all mad here, aren't we?'

'Sorry, Rim, but no, Zoé is a sensitive paranoid. She's one of those people who think they're never appreciated for their true worth. She's a murdered Mozart!'

'I don't know what you're talking about, Anna.'

'Saint-Exupéry came up with it. Go and look it up on Wikipedia, educate yourself.'

'No thanks.'

'You haven't lived with her.'

'No, and I don't plan to.'

Two minutes of silence followed, during which we pretended to look at the stars. Then, in a sort of competition for the worst contribution to the conversation, and perhaps also to lend some weight to her savage diagnosing of Zoé, Anna put on a surprise birthday party kind of voice to announce that she would soon be starting a course of psychoanalytic training. She had, without telling us, applied and been accepted to a prestigious institution. This cut me deep. Psychoanalysis was our common interest. She and I had been sharing a Google Doc for the past five years in which we wrote down our dreams (nothing is more boring than other people's dreams, but we purported to love each other enough to read one another's). The idea that one or the other of us would end up having patients lie down below a faded Kandinsky poster had been a joke between us for years. Right then, I realised how unpleasant it is when a shared pipe dream changes status for the person you've been dreaming with. What's more (and I know Rim was thinking the same thing), I was sure Anna would make a terrible analyst. She wouldn't have the patience to wait for her subjects' subconsciouses to wash up on the shore. On the contrary, she has an urgent desire to know everything about everyone (like Dr Krokowski in *The Magic Mountain*, whose sensitivity comes from the things that others don't tell him, rather than what they do). Though Rim and I should have been happy for her – our friend was making the leap from advice to action, from knowledge to risk – my eyes began to blink rapidly and my mouth to slowly open. Anna was waiting for my reaction, her head tilted to one side. I felt Rim on my side when I started talking again, to say sarcastically: 'Oh, you're one of *those* patients!' I sniggered: 'Ever heard of transference neurosis? For the cure to come to an end, the analyst has to be overthrown, and you, instead of letting the whole thing go, you take their armchair... It's a way of never letting it end.'

The charged silence that followed made me feel ashamed. Her eyes fixed on the table, Anna asked: 'And why would you want it to end, if you like it?' Her argument – so *shrink*-y – irritated me to the greatest possible degree; I downed my glass of red and declared that it was time for me to go and sort out the salade niçoise I was in charge of. Standing by the fridge, I was all the more angry with myself as the salad, made with no fresh ingredients, looked so pathetic. My only-child syndrome, i.e. an incapacity to do (for others) things that you judge (for yourself) to be pointless, would be revealed again. I tried to jazz it up a bit by giving it a good toss.

When I went back out, five minutes later, I was relieved to hear them laughing. The good mood had returned and it was as I sat down that I realised that it was at my expense. The target changes too quickly around here, I thought. It was another classic of our trio, a scene played out a hundred times: Anna and Rim were congratulating themselves on having only had one child.

Rim (to me as I was serving the salad): 'I dream of the patience you need to have more than one. When I see you with your boys, I realise I'm not cut out for that. It's like seeing someone do an entirely different job to mine.'

Me: 'Well, it's not like I have any particular talent. I'm the same as you.'

Rim: 'No, I swear you're more suited to it! The self-sacrifice… Personally I'd rather play the piano.'

Anna: 'Yes! Or read!'

Me: 'I read too!'

Rim: 'You read because you make yourself read. But there are some mothers who let everything slide. Their children become an excuse to do nothing else. Not take any career risks, for example.'

Me: 'Whereas you, on the other hand, take loads.'

Rim: 'What's that supposed to mean?'

Me: 'Give me one example of a risk you've taken recently! Did you move your mixing deck under the window?'

Anna: 'No need to be aggressive, Armelle. Rim's talking about the women who let their children become the alpha and omega of their lives.'

Me: 'Is that so bad? What, we don't like those women? And do they necessarily have two children?'

Anna: 'Yes, or three or four. By definition.'

Me: 'Sorry, but I think that's ridiculous. Maybe it's just your way of resisting the enormous social pressure to have two, but I'm telling you it's ridiculous.'

Anna: 'You can't deny that the more children you have, the less time you have for reading, writing, composing, making macramé.'

Me: 'I don't know about that. Maybe for a while. It goes in cycles. When you have two, they play together. It depends on the father too. And I'd say it's not worth artificially splitting everyone into two camps: the world of bohemian mothers of one and the other of stupid, submissive mothers of more. That's so annoying.'

All the more annoying was that, though I would have rather died than admit it, I could see what Rim and Anna were trying to say: the second child changes the gradient of the slope – to steeper. And as an aside, I was remembering a scene from a few days before we left for Louët. Lev, my five-year-old son, was in the bath playing with a rubber glove filled with water, while I was cooking rice for Gustave, his older brother, who was moaning from hunger as if his stomach were full of holes. Keeping an eye on the pot of water above my head, I was on my knees in front of the tumble dryer, which was vomiting children's underwear onto my lap, wondering if it was really necessary to sort them, or if at the end of the day, like with socks, the size of underwear doesn't matter that much and it always fits. Then I remembered my knickers on the school trip, and made two little piles. I listened out for drowning noises from the little one in the bathroom; shouted to the big one to eat a baguette: 'Whole, in one go, like a sword-swallower!' On the floor, I counted up the tasks to be completed: the rice, the bath, the remaining laundry on the floor in their bedroom. Dinner for them both, the crumbs, the table to be cleared. The big one's bath, the big one's homework. Pyjamas for them both, tooth-brushing for them both, ten minutes in bed for the little one, his reappearance in the living room, his glass of water sipped slowly, his smile because he's going to ask for something else. I thought back to my logistics class at university. *In what order should these issues be tackled? And if I started with the glass of water, what would happen on both a personal and global level?* With two children, I had mathematically increased this profoundly domestic time. Or, to put it another way, I had exacerbated the domestic concentricity: inside one task, another, smaller task was always waiting. The housework and the kitchen were like two obsessive tax inspectors that would never leave me alone. I had traded a carefree life for a family. A family, that is: an atmosphere, movement, complicity, a generous energy that flows through everything. Perhaps a family does hold your intellectual time at gunpoint, I thought, but it keeps you sharp in other ways.

During the hour that followed, we talked about the magazine and the cuts they'd made to the review space for theatre and classical music. Here at least we were all basically in agreement. Then, at ten-thirty, after Rim had unwrapped the cling film from her home-made brownies and handed out paper plates that Anna had given a disgusted, environmentally conscious look, the conversation returned to our children despite ourselves. Rim announced that she was going to sign her daughter up to the conservatoire next year, which annoyed me out of a Neuilly reflex, even though I had thought about doing the same thing. Then, despite ourselves, it turned to the 'genius' theme. Among friends, the temptation to present your children as gifted is strong: the younger they are, the fewer objective facts can contradict you and the more the poetry of childhood seems brilliant. It mustn't be overlooked, either, that the child's intuition is to say or do what they know will impress their parents – the key to assessing their intelligence is to ask yourself if the outside world also perceives them as such, enough to comment on it, which is rarely the case. Even if objectively I know all that, I was the first to celebrate my sons' miracles of inventiveness. 'Last summer,' I boasted, 'Lev said to me, "Having two friends on the beach is like balancing two pebbles on your back." That's lovely, isn't it?' Seamlessly, Rim shot back: 'Aloïs is already reading independently in reception.'

After a while, the conversation got stuck and became ridiculous to the point of torture. Soon our children would be speaking Chinese with their heads underwater. To put an end to it, I collected the glasses. Rim and Anna got to their feet. Piled up in the kitchen sink, the dirty plates were driving the flies on the sticky tape crazy, so Rim started to wash them up 'out of respect'. I dried up and Anna put away.

*

Sitting here on my balcony, I see that silent washing-up team again and reflect that our conversations about our children were rarely pleasant. Parenthood transforms us. Children give birth to parents: new adults, more materialistic, more conservative, whose horizons have retracted and whose internal batteries are low. The unbearable thing is that other parents don't see the same issues we do. While Anna, Rim and I hadn't changed too drastically when we became mothers, our friendship never managed to encompass the full spectrum of parenthood, and consequently our conversations about our children were always boobytrapped and unpleasant. Our children, the bearers of our differences, didn't get on so well. Seeing them interact was embarrassing. Wasn't that the proof that we didn't love each other any more?

*

The kitchen clock struck midnight as Rim finished the washing-up. Going upstairs to my bedroom, a little tipsy, I missed a step halfway up and slid all the way back down on my belly. *Bam bam bam* went my drunken body: a fall lacking any fighting spirit. Legs sore, flat on the floor, I raised my head towards Rim and Anna, who were coming out of the kitchen. I felt a pain spreading between my chest and my thighs. The girls were frozen to the spot, biting their lips. 'It's okay,' I said, 'nothing's broken, go ahead,' and a huge burst of laughter rang through the house. They came over to me, picked me up. Once we were sitting on the bottom step, pressed against each other, the Tunisian breeze caught us. I felt their warmth and my love for them returning.

'You fell for no reason,' said Rim, giggling.

I put an arm round her and the other round Anna. 'Look at us, Dr March's three drunk girls.'

'There were four of them,' Anna corrected me. 'We're more like Chekhov's three sisters when everything falls apart. We know we'll never go back to Moscow and that our brother will wind up as a little provincial apparatchik. We'll be forty soon, the age when you can't do anything else about who you are.'

'All you can do is accept it,' said Rim.

'Three sisters confronted with the principle of reality,' I put in.

'"Time goes and it seems all the while as if I am going away from the real, the beautiful life, farther and farther away, down some precipice,"' Anna recited. My friend delivered another line from memory, when Masha, the middle sister, says that her husband seemed impressive and intelligent at the start of their relationship. 'But it's not the same any more, alas.' Impressed by Anna's memory and the image of the unknown precipice, Rim and I let her 'alas' whistle through the hallway. I made the point that our lives had gone better than Masha's. Her hands on her cheeks, Anna admitted it: 'Yes, we're getting by all right.' Then she suggested we go to the top of the lighthouse to see the moon from closer up.

By the light of our phones, we got as far as the patio's back gate, which gave access to the other part of the island, just behind the house, before realising that it was closed off by two chains that looked like they came from a nuclear power plant. The silhouette of the lighthouse rose high in the night. Its flash lit up our faces intermittently. The moon was full. The rocks were desolate, black and wet. Some of them looked like huge faces in profile. I thought of the moor in Conan Doyle's *The Hound of the Baskervilles* and an ancient terror resurfaced. I wasn't so upset that we couldn't access the lighthouse. Up there, the guard rail was low and things could unravel, given the shitty evening we'd had. Rim said we should have a smoke to make ourselves feel better, and took three cigarettes from her packet of Winston Blues. 2005 called, it wants its cigarettes back, I commented to myself. Standing in an isosceles triangle, we took drags in silence. In the short term, it was less dangerous.

4

A Wrong Turn

When I woke the next morning, there was no noise upstairs and I had a sore throat from my one cigarette the night before. I massaged my neck, ruminating on the physical repercussions of a single smoke. I contemplated my oversized pyjama T-shirt with a gorilla's face on it, bought at Beauval Zoo back when it wasn't yet problematic to go to the zoo. I love it. I don't regret going. I dragged myself out of bed, as far as the window, where the view let me down. A curtain of grey sky smothered all the features of the landscape. You couldn't tell green from brown. Happy nonetheless to have woken early enough to get the house, particularly the kitchen, to myself for a while, I pulled on my jeans from the day before and noiselessly went downstairs. I opened the wooden shutters and hooked them to the outside wall so they wouldn't bang and wake the girls. But five minutes later, my solitude was shattered (as it so often is) by Rim, who came and joined me by the coffee machine, looking (as she so often does) like a drowsy Béatrice Dalle. Pod technology having overridden my ability to use a filter, I gave her an interrogative look. Yes, of course she still knew how to make coffee.

With our cups in hand, we went outside to walk around the house and, for the first time since we'd left for Louët, I wondered whether to tell her about my screenplay. She's too sleepy right now, I thought, reconsidering, before a host of other reasons came to mind. I thought about how the film wasn't finished, how it would undergo a thousand alterations before shooting, some of which would take it in a favourable direction, i.e. in a direction which distanced the narrative from our friendship. So instead I asked her favourite question: what was she listening to at the moment? Without hesitation, Rim sang a tune from *Rigoletto*. *Papam, papam, papam, papam, papam, papam, papam.* Far off, the sun was rising like a veiled coin. My childhood friend was also wearing a T-shirt from a gift shop – NIAGARA FALLS – under her orchestra conductor's jacket. A star-shaped sequin, probably a leftover from an outdoor festival, glittered on her neck, white and smooth like a baby's. Even though smoking in the morning was no longer the done thing at our age, she lit a cigarette with shaking hands. A third of her coffee spilled on the ground.

Around the back of the building, we stopped by a patch of hydrangeas, their once pink flowers now dried up. We were at the foot of a gravel path that climbed steeply to the highest point of the island but was barred halfway up by two big red plastic signs, CLIMBING NOT PERMITTED and DANGER OF LANDSLIDE. I pointed out to Rim that in the absence of security cameras or arranged marriages with a local Bluebeard (as it happened, I would find out later that there had been one called the Count of Conomor), it seemed to me that we could break that rule. We were alone on the island; the path wasn't slippery. A panoramic view, like a shot from *Planet Earth*, awaited us up there. More than actually being brave, I was seized by that *once-in-a-lifetime opportunity* feeling: the words *now or never* struck me like two blows to the face, the lack of phone signal all but forgotten. But I was waiting for a response from Rim, who was the Minister of Sports of our relationship. After brief consideration, she said: 'Out of the question – you're crazy. There wouldn't be two signs if there wasn't a real danger.' Her point about the number convinced me. Then her eyes roamed over my forehead, my too-big forehead, and that reminded me of an adventure from our childhood.

We were in Courchevel, skiing with her parents, and who knows, might still have not been far from them. Rim had gone off too quickly, a missile crashing down to earth, and I had followed her, flat out. In ten minutes, we had left her family and other Alpine life far behind. The pine trees were silent. The sky came right down to the ground, the same as that day on the island; by this point we had come to a stop and, from an aeroplane flying over the valley, our two silhouettes must have looked like neon figurines sticking out of the fog. Further down on our right, if we squinted, we could make out the contours of our chalet building. But Rim didn't want to go across the off-piste section that would take us back to the right path.

'Let's go and be very careful,' I said.

'No way. Read the sign.'

It was hard to believe, but she then gave me the order to follow her the wrong way. That is, to the left. And as she waited for me to reply, her eyes started to move frenetically over my forehead. This sign of stress, along with the extra month of life she had on me, brought me around.

'Okay, Rim, but we're taking the first button lift we see.' So, against all logic, we turned our back on our ski resort to get as far away from it as possible, to go in the opposite direction. As we went, the gentle descents gave way to cross-country skiing pistes and after an hour, out of breath, we ended up surrounded by mud. No more snow to speak of. Our Rossignol ski blades scraped at the first contact with the tarmac. *Crrrrrr.* Soon after, we took off our little skis, slung them over our shoulders and walked for twenty minutes, until the hard facts hit me. Firstly, the mountains on the horizon had become unrecognisable. The most likely explanation: we had crossed into a different valley. Next, the few chalets we could see above us were unreachable. Finally, the car parks were all empty and there were no ski lifts to be seen. It was at the sight of a tractor that I really started to panic. *That's not a vehicle for the mountains.* I sat on the floor and hit the ground with my blue mittens, which made no noise at all. Then, seeing that Rim was carrying on, I ran to catch up, leaped in front of her and sent the leftover bits of snow on my clothes flying everywhere. A dazzling choreography that I hoped wouldn't stop her from hearing the content of what I was saying, which was impressive for my ten years. I shouted that you couldn't decide everything when you got so many things wrong.

'My kidneys hurt. I can't walk any more. We're going to starve to death! Do you even realise, you lunatic, how close we were to our building?'

Rim raised an eyebrow. 'Come on, you look ridiculous when you cry. And you don't even know where your kidneys are.'

With my neon-pink outfit and astronaut gait, I didn't need to cry to look ridiculous. I walked with my skis crossed in my arms. In the end I was walking – or falling forwards, that was up for debate – but I looked like a player on *It's a Knockout* in the middle of a challenge. Or a mother trying to pull her child away from a merry-go-round. I kept my mouth firmly shut, determined not to say another word to her. And then finally, on a road so flat, straight and devoid of any sign of the cold that it could have been in Champagne-Ardenne, we wound up crossing the path of a beekeeper, rather than a paedophile looking for prey to tie up in his jet ski garage. The man, who looked to be in his sixties, was wearing plastic gloves, but not to strangle us. A stroke of luck. In a forest ranger kind of voice, he asked us if everything was okay. I rushed towards him and, deciding to opt for complete trust, declared us lost. *Better to put my life in his hands than to follow that madwoman for a second more.* 'Ah, okay, your parents must be very worried. Come with me,' he said, turning towards an American pickup truck. My mind immediately went to Clint Eastwood: were we going to sit in the back like adventurers? Unfortunately not; your luck could turn, yes, that could happen, but rarely to such extremes. The man showed us two spots next to the driver's seat. Then he drove us back to the French ski school at our resort, hugging all the bends in the road. The journey took about half an hour. Her head resting on the window, Rim sang along with Les Rita Mitsouko on the local radio in her deep, husky voice and I felt like killing her. How dare she? At the ski school, we sucked on pieces of ice taken from our ski boots while her family was located.

Quarter of an hour later, the arrival of Rim's father put an end to this delight of the senses. In the space of a second, Jean-Jacques had spotted us, grabbed us and dragged us by the biceps to the hire car, arms held above the shoulders as if stuck in the second phase of the butterfly stroke, our four neon legs running behind him. During this physical exertion, the smell of mulled wine that emanated from him left me baffled. *Let's take the edge off, warm ourselves up a bit, Emmanuelle, kids always find their way back eventually.* On the way over to our chalet building, I felt sick at the thought of the telling-off that was sure to come from this Claude Brasseur in a black snowsuit (I had in mind the painful memory of when, in the garden of a Center Parcs villa, overexcited and tired out after a day spent with Rim in the wave pool, I'd thrown a stone – for a laugh or simply for something to do – and it had landed an inch from his skull. Jiji had pounced on me, pinched my cheeks between his fingers and squeezed hard, while with the wisdom of all my eight years I tried to explain to him through my tears that he hadn't, as he kept yelling, 'had a lucky escape', because any other random throw would have resulted in a different trajectory).

In Jiji's car, I was also afraid that he would confiscate my pocket money, which was considerable that year thanks to a miscalculation on my parents' part. In the seat in front of me, Rim was looking out of the window, worried. At least she wasn't singing any more. And then, once we were in the lift, there was a setback: press like a madman as Jean-Jacques might on the button for our floor, the metal doors wouldn't close. He said 'shit' and 'fuck' and 'shit' again; it didn't change a thing. He pressed hard, and gently. After a couple of seconds, our frustrated children's eyes, roving around the lift, naturally ended up meeting. *Bam.* A tiny meeting before continuing their routes, but a tiny meeting that was enough to send our throats up in flames like young pine trees. Tears in the corners of our eyes, our lips, everywhere else. Shaking inside. His back to us, Jean-Jacques pretended not to hear the spasms, the gasping for breath, the suffocating, the twin epileptic fits going on behind him. Was he laughing too? When the lift abruptly took off (as if, after a lot of thought, yes, all right then, it agreed to go up; it was even a resounding yes), we all had to find a position to avoid falling over. Rim grabbed on to my knees and I spread over her back, her head in my stomach. Two drunkards holding each other up at the break of day. When we got to our floor, Jiji rushed out of the lift and Rim and I spent twenty minutes sitting on the black duckboard in the corridor, trying to calm down. Then we made our entrance to the living room that doubled as her parents' bedroom at night and a barn during the day (that wasn't true, but it was my joke of the holidays – I've always found the Barbie-caravan aspect of these ski resorts funny). Feverish but dignified, we were expecting, mistakenly, to be able to sit and watch our favourite game show on TV. It was about to come on. But with a wave of her hand, Emmanuelle sent us to bed.

Heading back towards the lightkeeper's cottage, I said to Rim, who takes recontextualisation as an insult: 'Remember back in the nineties, when we had to go without TV and a nice raclette because of your inflexibility about signage?' She smiled and replied that maybe she would climb up to the top of the island with me, but later in the day. She'd think about it, she promised.

On the patio, the breakfast table looked straight out of Goldilocks and the Three Bears. Anna had put out round brioche rolls on little plates decorated with triskelions, and filled our glasses with what appeared to be organic apple juice (cloudy, in any case). As we approached, I felt obliged to tell her we'd only been gone five minutes: 'You were still asleep… We just walked around the house, nothing exciting.' But my prudence was pointless, Anna didn't care, she was inspecting a beach on the mainland with some plastic binoculars she'd found in a toy box in the living room. Her attention was focused on an older couple.

'The woman with purple hair has her arm around her husband's shoulders. They're up to their knees in the water. They haven't moved in several minutes. If we're like them when we're old, the most loved-up couple on the beach, then frankly, everything will be all right.'

Having a look myself, I made out a crutch behind the woman's right leg. The sort that Rim and I had dreamed of in Neuilly, so on trend were they after the winter holidays. Then, seeing a bit better the way the pair were balancing, I realised that the husband was acting as a complementary piece of medical equipment for his wife. An old man object, an old man who might have rather been basking in the sun with a group of pensioners in Thailand but who was there, under his wife's armpit.

I put down the binoculars on the garden wall. The ruthless strength of our subjectivities depressed me. If a scene like that could be interpreted in such different ways by Anna and by me, what were we talking about when we talked to each other?

Discords

The weather was grey, but mild enough to have breakfast outside. At the table, we scrolled silently on our phones despite having no signal. Rim's slurps of apple juice disgusted me as much as her way of eating spaghetti had when we were kids. In that aspect, Rim hadn't grown up; she always ate as if her stomach was ordering her to. This awoke an old anxiety: that our stomachs are the real masters of the world and all the rest of our bodies – legs, hair, eyes – is nothing but an apparatus so that they can reproduce. I resisted the urge to scold her and managed to concentrate on the story she was telling. She was talking about a sex party that sounded like a pornographic fairy tale. In front of a succession of naturalistic backdrops (branches, prairie, bushes), she and Niels had had sex with people of all shapes and sizes. Men and women indiscriminately. This was the radical idea they'd had to spice up their sex life, which they set about doing under the influence of ecstasy because, in their usual state, Rim couldn't bear being touched and Niels was too shy. This party had been their first foray into it and what she was describing was much too sordid for Anna and me, who only had two or three sexual positions in our repertoire, but we listened with curiosity because sex had become an issue for us too. With age, the cost-to-benefit ratio of the whole thing had changed. Among my female friends, there were some who had come to terms with not fucking any more. The same way you stop going clubbing at some point, they said: 'Okay, that's it, enough contortion now.' So we listened to her attentively. From my point of view, irony didn't rear its head until Rim started to paint these orgies as political activism. These gang bangs were portrayed as an anti-racist and anti-capitalist process, when in reality they didn't achieve anything more than a winter trip to Guadeloupe would. 'Sorry, Rim, but drugs and outdoor sex have never saved the world... You know Yoko Ono lives in a neocolonial villa in Palm Beach?' I asked, struck in that same instant by regret for our childhood dreams. Rim and I had planned to do big things, to invent vaccines, and in the end we'd accomplished nothing. A bit of music and film, some desk journalism, but the greatest achievement to our names was the creation of two polluting family units.

In the time it took me to set aside our Pasteurian aspirations and rejoin the conversation, Rim had moved on to a new story. A few days before the sex party, she had attended a private gig in the Paris catacombs. After following a path marked with chalk arrows through a damp corridor, she had danced in candlelit caverns and ended the night sitting in her own vomit. Anna was smiling politely, looking off into the distance. I didn't make the same effort; I was hearing this anecdote for the second time, and the 'party scene' that Rim talked about so often irritated me with its way of judging people solely on how they appear in that present moment. *Never mind the merits of what you do on Monday mornings.*

I said:

'Being the queen of all these cool parties must make up for all the bullying we endured at school.'

'That's not why I do it,' she replied.

After breakfast, we put our deckchairs on the edge of the patio, where the border wall fell sharply into the sea. Anna put up her feet on its rim and we copied her. She was wearing a white T-shirt and tartan trousers, her blonde hair tucked under a straw hat. Rim took off her black jacket and I discovered she had a new tattoo on her forearm. She raised her eyes to the sky, and I followed her gaze. Above the island, clouds passed as fast as lorries on the motorway. I was sitting in the middle. To my right, Anna was reading *Philosophie Magazine* and to my left, Rim was still singing to herself, which would have been annoying if the sound of the water hadn't been even more so. The lapping of the waves was wearing me down.

There's an Iris Murdoch novel, *The Sea, the Sea*, which takes place on the other side of the Channel. It tells the story of a big name in the London theatre world who retires to an isolated little village on the English coast. One day in the street, he sees his childhood sweetheart, who left him when they were young adults without him ever knowing why. Seeing her fragile and having lost her looks, he thinks she must be desperate and destitute, full of regret and still madly in love with him. He's so convinced of it that the reader believes it too, even though nothing the woman says or does implies anything of the sort. This brilliant book makes us complicit in its hero's erotomania; only his impatience towards the sea allows us to glimpse his extreme neurosis. In front of his house, the waves suck at the corners of the cove before ebbing noisily. Although he never could have imagined it would do so, this becomes a burden on the narrator's spirit. Deep down, I was just as anxiety-ridden as him.

Rim stopped humming and I sensed that she wanted me to ask her more questions about her wild nights, but I didn't feel like it. Conversations between friends can sometimes take an altruistic turn (*I'm going to broach that annoying subject because I feel like she needs me to, and then later I'll be able to talk about that thing she's sick of hearing about*). But in the crisis our friendship was going through, that ruse wasn't going to work any more.

I tried to fall asleep by counting the heads of the Film department appointed since I'd arrived at the magazine (a cursed position that everyone failed in, because occupying it meant passing off your own tastes as objective reality). As I emerged from my siesta, I heard Anna retelling one of our historic disagreements in a low voice. A strange thing to do. Forgiveness is a dialogue and the resolution of a conflict as precarious as a property deal; the grey areas have been voluntarily set aside, by both parties, as a show of good intentions.

As it happens, the scene Anna was describing had happened more than a year beforehand. Coming back from an assignment, we had been caught up in a riot near the Champs-Élysées; projectiles and smoke bombs were flying over our heads. I had wanted to film it for the magazine's website, but Anna pulled me away by the arm. Once we were back at the office, I'd recounted how she'd run away. I'd described her panic; I'd even imitated her. 'She took me hostage and then walked all over me. There was a bit of class disdain to it too. She made me out to be a Heidi who comes down from the mountains and can't stand the violence of the city,' Anna was telling Rim. 'She treated me like a doll whose hair you style by pulling her head backwards. As if I didn't have the ability to feel pain,' she added as red blotches appeared on her forehead (I was watching her through my eyelashes).

I couldn't believe what I was hearing. How could something so trivial still be on her mind after all this time? By the way, the part Anna wasn't telling was that several days later, seeing as she was still sulking (she'd carried on asking me questions but wouldn't answer any of mine), I had called her out: 'Okay, that'll do, spit it out already.' I'd then received a barrage of insults and swearing over my head. The disproportionate rage she had surely wanted to spare me came surging to the surface like molten lava. Although she'd clarified that the things she was angry about were already of the past, they clearly weren't dead yet either. I came out of it shattered by anger at both of us, and I didn't call her for a whole month, and I missed her. Because Anna has always played the role of a drainpipe for my daily observations. It's part of my cerebral plumbing, and it's essential.

For me, her mind was like a second brain that the first one could offload onto. Really, it was an intellectual friendship. The sort that lets you explain something to the other person and elucidate it for yourself at the same time. Without her, I fell into panoramic sorts of conversations, friendly chit-chat, *How is Whatshisname and what's going on with your friend Thingy McWhatsit?* Conversations with no altitude.

We'd been getting out of sync for a while. Our latest disagreement had been about a month before Louët. To sum up, Anna's little sister, who'd come to Paris to study, had fallen in love with a guy who lived on the same floor of her building and who – small world – happened to be one of my first cousins. An unbearable Breton who used to swear, when I was little, that my mother was 'a whore who would die in a car crash'. What the connection was between those two assertions, I never knew. When she heard the news, Anna, whose knowledge of my family is encyclopedic, felt it was urgent to pull the wool from this silly little twenty-five-year-old's eyes. She set up a dinner where my tacit role was to demolish the boy. That evening, I spoke with terrifying fervour. I strung together the worst anecdotes, cruel memories and more recent things too, and in doing so I set off a series of small earthquakes inside that young woman. It was a pointless torture, since these sorts of arguments don't make you stop loving someone. That never happens. On the contrary, the criticism makes your internal defences flare up. It's psychologically exhausting, but the image of the one you love is reinforced whatever the cost. The young woman opposite me had trouble keeping up. Her skin turned the colour of her panna cotta. Across the table, Anna seemed to contain twice as much blood as her sister. More than anything, she was thrilled to have carried out her sisterly duties by showing her, via me, the right path to follow. 'Letting your loved ones make a mess of things has never been a sign of affection,' she would often say. *And that's the limit of the powers of your understanding*, I would reply in my head. *You have to let things run their course*. There are just as few reasons to love as there are to stop loving. These things play out somewhere beyond our understanding. You can love someone simply for their funny way of opening their arms for you to nestle into. That night, frustrated by her way of conducting our friendship so forcefully, I made a mental list of everything I'd had enough of. At the top: it was time to get rid of our shared fifty-page Google Doc. It had been going for five years, our file modestly titled *The Interpretation of Our Dreams*, and it was the proof of our psychological fusion, our teenage co-dependency. A lack of serious boundaries. I deleted it soon afterwards, pretending it was a user error, and ever since then I'd been dreaming that I put my secrets inside balloons that I inserted into the stomachs of stray cats.

To be clear, I felt a physical urge to escape Anna's general influence. Her director's chair. A brilliant but intrusive spin doctor, she reminded me of the psychoanalyst Conrad Stein, who doesn't want his readers to emerge intact from his thought. Every conversation left its mark on me. I would need, after Louët, to stop consulting her on every little thing. I would suggest that she do some 'self-coaching' instead. We needed to stop discussing our anxieties together because we no longer knew, at the end of the day, what came first: the discussion about anxiety or the anxiety about discussion. Hearing her recount this old argument made me want to yell *Don't you realise how heavy your demands are? I'd like to be able to tell you things you don't like hearing without the risk of unleashing Neptune's wrath.* I was afraid of her buried rage and I didn't like being criticised, much less when it had become a grudge. I was pissed off with Rim too for not coming to my defence. *They can both go fuck themselves.* I didn't need them – quite the opposite. I got up off my deckchair and said: 'Nice idea to tell that story, Anna, but as I've heard it before, I'm going to make myself a cup of tea.'

Once in the kitchen, to console myself, I thought about the waves coming in my professional future. Good ones. Everything was going to go well for me; I had stopped keeping my ambitions intact by avoiding any actual realisation of them, and I'd set to work.

My first short film had received several awards and I'd finally signed on to make a feature-length with a big production company. The place was so impressive that I'd been scared I'd suddenly develop Tourette's, that I'd throw all the pages up in the air and insult everyone, but in the end it was okay; I drank a glass of water and everything went fine. Filming was due to take place in two years' time, the casting of the main characters in a few months. I wouldn't become a psychoanalyst, but I was going to carve out my own path. As it happened, I was planning to tell them over pre-dinner drinks that very evening that I was leaving the magazine. I would say: 'Well, it's happening – I'm starting my second life.' Rim and Anna would be emotional, and yes, a little bit jealous.

But that self-celebration was stopped in its tracks when I went past the open window. Outside, Anna had started criticising my one existing film. Apparently my film-making was technically interesting but fell prey to the same self-centredness I'd displayed that day on the Champs-Élysées. My artistic process consisted of casting those close to me in my little Punch and Judy theatre. Through my intimate screenplays, I had found a new way of exercising my individualism, of appropriating other people's best ideas and giving myself the starring role. More generally, she had more and more trouble with writers who put their selves out into the world in a thousand different forms, in a perpetual dialogue with themselves, as Julien Gracq would put it, when there are pressing political matters. A green dictatorship to set up, for example.

I sat down next to the sticky tape and tried as hard as I could not to take it too badly. For one thing, I wasn't one of these trapped flies; I had a future and I could be pleased about that. I entered negotiations with my teacher's-pet syndrome. I reasoned: 1. My films were autofictional (they had their roots in real events, but their narrative framework was fictional). 2. Even if they had been autobiographical, it's possible to do that with dignity. In his *Memoirs of an Egotist*, Stendhal takes himself as the subject of analysis, and is aware that vanity constitutes a threat ('What I am writing seems rather boring to me; if this continues, this won't be a book but an examination of conscience'). 3. For me, the process consisted of injecting my own experiences into a story the way others insert historical facts or a moral. And after that, it was all a matter of proportions, then of camouflage, but no creation can escape experience. So was it narcissism, navel-gazing, exhibitionism, disengagement with politics? No, I thought, not when the work has been done to elaborate on it. And the difficulty is the measure of it. But then Anna added: 'I'm not feeling good about what's coming next. Armelle thinks her sort of slightly twisted charm will let her get away with anything. She'll end up writing about us.' The lucidity of this criticism took my breath away.

My anxiety rose. What was she going to think about my project? A month earlier, my psychoanalyst had retired and I hadn't looked for a replacement, thinking that I was in a good, functional state, and that my professional transition would confirm this. In truth, the end of my journalism career, and what I was producing, exactly, as a *film-maker of the intimate* had left me fragile. My incessantly exteriorised interiority blurred the boundaries between reality and fantasy. I no longer knew to whom or to what my creative process was indebted. I no longer knew who my characters were, them or me or both, if I needed to apologise and to whom. Anna had hit the nail on the head. Since I'd made the decision to quit, my doubts had been taking up all the space in my head and you could even say that a historic valve had burst. The many tasks that needed doing to survive without a salary were flapping their wings in my face. The panic attacks from my teenage years resurfaced, serious ones, the sort that make your neck tense up and squeeze your heart to the point that you have to hug your sides tight to fall asleep. I was plagued by intrusive thoughts (the fear of killing my loved ones with an axe or a milk bottle). And feelings of unreality, out-of-body experiences. This island wasn't helping at all. I had to forget about the impossibility of escape. Breathe gently and inhale what had just been exhaled. Calm down, like when the lights go out at the opera and you can't get up any more without disturbing ten other people. I breathed like that and, half an hour later, I was no longer shaking and the girls had changed topic. Through the window, the sky and the sea formed a silvery whole. I accepted that I was going to have to return to the patio along with all the ridicule that going back to a situation you've stormed out of entails. I made my tea, drank half and went back out of the house.

As I approached Rim and Anna, they were talking about Tunisia. Rim admitted that she still read everything written by and about Raphaël. She preferred celebrity magazines to his books – his books were so ridiculous. The guy thought he was Malraux. Physically, with his menacing look, he more and more resembled Pete Doherty, she said.

'Given the choice of scandalous Brits, we'd all rather go for Jude Law,' I commented. Rim smiled.

'You're both crazy. If we really get to choose, it's Laurence Olivier,' Anna cut in.

This welcome immediately softened me. *It's normal for tensions to arise when you're spending several days together.* I suggested we fold up our deckchairs and move around a bit – as much as the island would allow.

6

Oblique Love

At noon, the grey curtain lifted. From the tip of the island, the view of the Taureau was astonishing. The air was so clear we could almost see inside the old prison cells in the fort. To our right extended Brittany's rugged coast, to our left stretched the open sea, and behind us stood, like a fourth person, a metal cross that came up to my chest. The year 1841 was cut into its trunk and a few paces beyond it, the island ended. How lucky to be buried there, I thought. It's better than Montmartre cemetery. The earlier tensions had evaporated and, in a light-hearted mood, I threw out some theories on the identity of the person buried there: 'Well, let's change it to the year 1941, okay? That's easier for a history dolt like me. Let's say that a plane crashed here one morning. The English officer died as the sun was rising.' Anna joined in: 'It's here that the wife of a prisoner in the Taureau committed suicide after reading a Rimbaud poem aloud. "Eternity". Eternity, it is the sea gone with the sun.' In a firm enough voice to put an end to the game, Rim said that it was a lightkeeper's grave, end of story, and we should leave it in peace. 'Poor

Rim's not sure that death's eternal – we shouldn't give her such harsh reminders,' I said, laughing. Rim ignored my jab, took a breath through the nose and mouth, blinked, and then suggested we come back to that spot for our famous pre-dinner drinks that evening. So far from the atmosphere of the ones we had under Djerba's fire sign, I thought. Glancing at me, she added that she'd brought Martini Bianco.

That's my favourite drink, and I would have felt content if it weren't for the presence of three herring gulls above me. One thing I hadn't taken into account about this trip: the seagulls. I hate them to the point of denying their existence. So, at that moment, they were rising as much from my sub-conscious as from their hiding place. We hadn't seen them when we arrived on the island because they reigned across the other side, the one looking out to sea. I leaned over to see how many there were and thought I was hallucinating – there were thousands of them, perched on this tragic, crumbling coast, shaped by the open sea. A colony. Dirty white. With beating hearts. The tip of the island, where we stood, was the beginning of their territory and so, since they don't mess around in the world of birds, two of them came and barred our way. They puffed out their necks and narrowed their eyes, grunting at us. When Rim took a step forwards, they let out a warning cry. They filled the sky, a dome of birds made of shrill malice. They nosedived towards us and the wind drove them back.

'Let's go back, it's dangerous,' I muttered.

'You're scared because one bit you on the bum when you were a kid,' Rim said.

'Exactly,' I replied, irritated.

'In front of my family, who laughed till they cried.'

'Indeed.'

'So you're not objective.'

'No, but I know what I'm talking about. Believe me, our only hope is that they're not nesting right now. They can rip your hair out.'

'What-ev-er,' said Rim, detaching the syllables. (I've never worked out if this expressive habit of Rim's masks tenderness, irritation or both. But this way of reading all my behaviour through the lens of three anecdotes from a thousand years ago bothered me deeply.)

While we'd been having this conversation, the situation had worsened. The dome was closing in on us, two dozen birds threatening us with piercing cries. A low-budget Hitchcock set in Brittany. Or maybe a Disney film, since on the ground a seagull was fighting its way through our feet. The overweight bird walked with its head held high, wiggling its backside and not looking at us. I hated that one too. To provoke this cowardly, violent, two-legged world, I said that we shouldn't eat anything there that evening: 'There won't be any crumbs of anything, pals.' I said it loud enough for the gull on the ground to hear me and think it over. Then, to make the girls laugh, I shouted at the sky: 'No salt and vinegar crisps for you!' The result: Anna and Rim didn't laugh, and they started walking away. On our way back to the cottage, I thought about the lightkeepers who had lived there for centuries with these ungrateful creatures. Had they learned to speak to them? And if so, in which libraries could their memoirs be found?

Going back past the signs forbidding access to the top of the island, I felt gloomy all of a sudden – too many restrictions on this island. I dragged my feet. It was 3 p.m. If I leave now, I'll get home at nine, I thought. It'll be perfect.

In the kitchen, Anna found a frozen Snickers bar at the back of the freezer. She ate it in three bites as she turned on an old floor lamp which was exactly the same height as her, then suggested we watch an old film on my MacBook. And she could plait my hair at the same time, if I was up for it. I said okay, I wouldn't mind that. It reminded me that Rim had loved me doing her hair when we were kids. I've already mentioned this – when sober, i.e. most of the time, my childhood friend has become averse to all physical touch. This happened, with no explanation, when she started secondary school. A negative magnetic field formed around her body. A natural authority emerged. In the end, she wouldn't let anyone approach except when high, drunk or afraid someone was going to cut her open. (One day, in the waiting room of an unaffordable dentist's on the Avenue de Wagram, when we were fifteen, she told me, with the intensity of someone uttering their last words, 'The idea of being opened up is unbearable.' I put my hands on either side of her face and rested my forehead against hers. Then we ran away.)

I put Woody Allen's *Crimes and Misdemeanors* into the DVD drive of my laptop, confusedly ashamed that I didn't start a conversation about the crime he was accused of by his adoptive daughter, Dylan, who actually appears in the final scene. I should really give up his films, or at least sign up to a list of people who are going to give up his films soon. Already sitting, I slid between Anna's knees and waited on the floor. My friends were playing 'Set the salary of people at the magazine'.

'And how much should we pay Paul, Anna?'

'Five hundred and eighty euros per month.'

'You're crazy!'

'He works like three hours a week. We haven't seen him in the office in a year.'

'You're right. Five hundred and eighty euros a month, that's what he deserves. Print media is in crisis.'

'He should leave Paris if it's too expensive for him.'

'He should move out near Disneyland, for fun as well. He can go on the teacups every day.'

'Further – he can go all the way to Château-Thierry. Fuck him,' Anna replied.

'Ooh, you're harsh,' I laughed.

'Yeah, and you're Mother Teresa.'

At 6 p.m. we went back to the tip of the island for our pre-dinner drinks, making as little noise as possible so as not to disturb the birds. Our shoes slid along the earthen path like mop slippers and, by some miracle, all was calm. The two guards had left their posts (slackers). On the other slope, the seagulls were still listening out for us, that was clear, but were now opting for the musical statues strategy. We sat down three metres from the edge, behind the metal cross from 1841. Looking over at it, I felt its indifference. It was decorated with an arabesque pattern, well planted in the ground, barely rusted. It was there. Just so. Undaunted and solid. Like the pebbles embedded in the ground, it would outlive us by a long time. The troubling thing, I thought, is that desert islands are like paintings. They lie outside the scope of human decisions. Everything is kept exactly the same; only the light changes. Or, to put it another way: we could time-travel a thousand years, in one direction or the other, and it wouldn't change anything we see. Here, the past and the future are mixed up. From here, time is that terrible thing that happens to other people, poor creatures of the mainland. If we stayed, would we get older?

Rim took out the Martini bottle from a thin plastic Monoprix bag. It was cold, she explained, from being outside all night. She poured some for Anna, then for herself, and me last. Her smile was tense and even strange (but I know that I've always focused on her mouth too much, so I archived the information). The first – very sweet – sip woke me up, and the second reminded me of the discomfort of the previous night. I would have liked to have been warned before we arrived that the toilets were outside the house; I might have rethought the whole thing. The worst part was that to get to them you had to climb a steep rock with the help of a length of nautical rope tied to who knows what at the top. Then you had to struggle through the brambles, crushing ants underfoot, and navigate a wooden door that wouldn't budge unless you forced it with the intent of breaking it into a thousand pieces. (*Oh, fuck it, I'll break it*.) After all that, on the way back, you'd have to rappel down the rock like you were canyoning. Before midnight, this rigmarole was still possible. But afterwards... No, to be honest it was all too scary. The rodents. The night a sheet of black Canson paper. The beam from the lighthouse intermittently exposing us to the telescopes on the mainland. Under my covers the night before, I'd wound up convincing myself that a zombie had occupied the top of the lighthouse for millennia. Given the tiny size of the island, the chase I had conceived in my head was comically small-scale. A macabre Tom and Jerry scene. To distract myself, I started to monitor my insides. Half-full at 1.24, it was bearable. The girls were asleep, their haemoglobin resting, while I surveyed the marginal volume of the hot-water-bottle-shaped vessel that I imagined my bladder to be. *But if I can't hold it, what then? Piss in the cast-iron casserole dish and wash it afterwards? The washing-up liquid is eco-friendly, though; will it actually clean it? And if I do that, will it set off something feral in me? Will I start pissing in casserole dishes as a rule? Who will want to have anything to do with me?*

To have a calmer night, I'd decided to stick to one well-filled glass of Martini Bianco. I warned them: 'I'm going to stick to one well-filled glass of Martini.' But they weren't listening, there was too much to see. Everything was painfully beautiful. The sun was bowing into the sea. It yielded, it flowed, it embraced the sea, it gave itself up completely. Its orange light melted over the surface and was projected forwards to give the grass at my feet an amber tint which – and this was the beautiful thing – didn't overwhelm the original green. As the wind was gently rising, the long stems moved as though they were playing Rim's Chopin. Then suddenly, the orangey-red hue vanished. Everything leaned towards the blue, the grey, became darker and more silvery, and the sea took on the aspect of a mirror made of ice. The light became metallic; I watched my friends looking off into the distance, and I remembered that I loved them in a way more oblique than the horizon, which looks different to everyone, since we each live in our own visual field.

7

I'd have quite liked to be friends with Lacan too

I contemplated Rim. The baby hair around her temples was curling in the humidity, and I thought that we were like two chiffon puppets trapped in a chest – or, on second thoughts, a sort of giant uterus (that's disgusting, sorry, but it's the image that came to mind). If one of us were to disappear, I thought, loneliness would strike the other in everything she did; even her movement would become weak and shaky. In a prophetic kind of way, I felt that her absence would send me into the jasmine-scented river, so rapid and sad, of depression. Our friendship wasn't perfect and wasn't really based on mutual understanding, but it was architecturally strong. We were pillars, structures, foundations for each other. Rim had helped me build myself on a family unit that had smashed on the floor. Actually, if we follow that with another image, it's like Rim and I met at the top of Annapurna. Crevasse twins. It was a matter of team spirit.

The love between Anna and me was more fragile. An enduring harmony, a running commentary on our lives, like

musical notes that follow each other. When I had put on
the DVD, before doing my plaits she'd gathered my hair
at the roots to lift it and divide it into sections. It gave me
shivers. There was the sensuality of it, and the fact that she
was talking so passionately about her latest discovery. As
she did my hair, she explained an American philosopher's
theory that you mustn't break off a relationship in a uni-
lateral way, because it's extremely violent to suddenly take
a part of the other person's identity away from them (the
part that resides in the 'us'). It's like an amputation. Medieval. In reality, everything can be resolved with a negotiation
of needs. 'Yeah, but there are some people who are happy
never to let go,' I replied, running the risk that she'd think
I was talking about her relationship with Adel, which was
true. A cheesy song about break-ups popped into my head
(*If you leave me now / You'll take away the biggest part of
me*), and the idea that no idea ever uttered is original, this
one included, occurred to me. Annoyed, Anna changed the
subject. She grabbed her phone to calculate my ACE – ad-
verse childhood experience – score. It's a system designed to
evaluate childhood trauma, she explained to me via a series
of questions ('Were you hit/humiliated by your parents?').
American research has shown that this score is correlated
to an individual's overall health as an adult. The right-hand
braid was finished; she started tackling the other side. Rim
was focused on the film, which was convenient for me answering the questions. I exaggerated the unhappiness of my
home life, and Anna, having surely done the same thing,
discovered that we had the same score: 4/10. 'Ah, I'm not

surprised, you know,' she said. 'We're not friends for nothing,' I added, the left side of my face covered with hair. So yes, I liked the depth and substance of these conversations, but the need to please her never gave me a second of peace.

The summer before, Anna had found herself alone in Paris. Panchi and their daughter had gone to sleep in a tent in a forest somewhere, and she couldn't bear to do that. 'Only profoundly middle-class people find that kind of thing fun.' After shutting the door behind them, she took a trip through all the empty rooms in her apartment, in every sense, and felt it as deeply as a sexual experience. To start with, you can hardly believe the silence, the solitude; it's too good to be true. But very quickly, within the hour, happiness turns into a realisation: you're not expected anywhere, no one's waiting for you. The terror of being confronted with yourself. The family apartment had lost its family; its function had been stripped away. By 7 p.m., when everyone is usually busying around, a feeling of emptiness was crushing my friend's chest. Were they all dead? Had she dreamed them? What to do? Get out of bed, pace around the apartment, yes, but what for? And why go into the living room rather than the bathroom? Sitting on her retro bathtub, Anna realised that for all her sudden freedom she had nothing to do other than eat vacuum-packed cucumbers and ask unavailable people out for coffee. She thought that she should have foreseen this, made sure she had things in the diary. She called me: 'Fucking hell, I don't have a life any more. I'm single and sexy, but for no one.'

I told her that the last time that had happened to me, being on my own in Paris, I'd wound up on the phone with my old sixth form boyfriend who now lived in Dubai, held some anti-France economic views and wouldn't stop asking me if I wanted to go and have a bath 'right now' while he stayed on the line. In the end I'd told him that while I wasn't entirely opposed to having phone sex with him, I thought he was too right-wing. After that, I swore off exercising my freedom, my urge to *take action*, and the rest of the week was more relaxing than ever. I fell into a regressive state that involved throwing Babybels into tubs of grated carrot and eating the result. I didn't wash anything up. I just piled it all around me. I lived surrounded by the corpses of Diet Cokes and in communion with Claude Sautet films. In the end, it gave me food for thought, but I didn't really miss anyone, and I was sure it would be the same for her.

Unconvinced, Anna asked if I wanted to come and have lunch at hers the next day. Although it was technically im-possible, I accepted wholeheartedly. That morning, I had a meeting with a painter for the magazine. Then I had to go and catch a train to join Daniel and the children in the Basque Country. Between these two obligations there was a hypothetical window of time that my friend grabbed hold of like a T-Rex. During the interview with the artist, I put my phone on flight mode. Coming out of the meeting, late and shaken up (the woman, who suffered from migraines that stopped her from working, had gestured incessantly with her hands like claw machines that never unfurled), I turned it back on. Three messages from Anna.

Are you still coming?
?
???

I gathered my courage over the course of three hundred metres and called her. She picked up and let a long silence fall. 'Hi Anna!' I explained it had been impossible for me to cut the meeting short ('Yesterday evening, she had to go to A & E to be put on a Laroxyl drip. Did you know, did you have any idea that people go to A & E with migraines?'). No, but it didn't surprise her. 'I don't understand. Didn't you know that they're painful?' Her tone was exasperated. She asked me what time my train was. '2.17 p.m. exactly.' A new, hellish silence; the phone line had never been more strained. Then she ended up taking pity on me. Tightly: 'I don't think it's really worth you coming to the house.' 'Oh, don't you think so?' I'd asked, pretending to find the idea a radical one. 'Yeah, look, you're probably right, but I can stay on the phone with you on the way to the station.' This suggestion was miraculously enough to appease her. She was going to have lunch with someone. Her voice got warmer and I started to hear domestic noises. She took a vegetable tart out of the oven (sound of the oven door), and got a plate and cutlery (sound of cutlery). Once seated at the breakfast bar in her American-style kitchen, she asked me for an update on my life (depending on the day, she would say 'Debrief' or 'Update!'). In those moments, she was the

CEO of a company and I was both the topic of business and the head of sales. I gathered up everything intelligent my mind had produced over the last few days. The phone was making my ear hot, which I hated.

'Where are you now?'

'At Gambetta Métro.'

'Go to Alexandre Dumas, it'll be easier.'

'Are you sure? Why?'

'The change will be quicker.'

'Okay, but are you sure it's worth the effort? Because it'll take me a while to get there... Right?'

'No, I swear you'll save time. This way, you won't even have to climb any stairs.'

'Okay, great.' (I couldn't care less about having to climb stairs.)

My greatest desire was to go into the station in front of me, but I couldn't piss her off any further. To get to Alexandre Dumas, nothing could be simpler, she'd told me; I only had to go along the edge of the Père-Lachaise cemetery. I'd furtively thought back to Manuel's text – *I love Père-Lachaise* – and decided that *I still didn't*. I spotted its outer wall ('Ah, yeah, I see it') and followed it at a trot while discussing the psychosomatic nature of migraines, and Freud, a migraine sufferer himself, with Anna, until I realised I didn't recognise Paris any more. More sky. Wider roads. Oh God, these were the outer boulevards, I wasn't going in the right direction at all. I took three more steps out of optimism. Coming face to face with a tramline, I interrupted her: 'Hang on a second, I think I'm lost.' I gave her the name of the road I was on, and then an adjoining one so that Google Maps would have the full picture. And it was hearing her swear in Savoyard ('good heavens above') that confirmed I'd been going the wrong way down the cemetery road (which won't always be the case). 'You're in the opposite place from where you should be,' she told me, irritated. 'Shit,' I replied, smacking my forehead with my palm. Then she advised me to run in the opposite direction, 'and fast', if I still wanted to make my train. Yes, I still wanted to make it. Nothing had changed. But instead I ran after a green firefly, gesturing wildly like someone who's just survived a disaster. Sitting in the taxi, I said with the determination I'd been lacking an hour earlier, 'Gare Montparnasse, please.'

The young driver had also let a silence fall (habit of the day). Then he stopped and started several times. The slightest awareness of my surroundings would have alerted me to the problem: the road was jammed; we wouldn't be going anywhere. Even the car itself had realised, and refused to move. But I was concentrating on Anna's imitation of her psychoanalyst's three different throat-clearing noises and I didn't decode the situation. The driver started his impossible journey and the two or three crucial actions that would have got me out of the predicament (getting out of the vehicle, for a start) didn't occur to me. I was engrossed in my friend's words. The taxi never got into third gear. After an hour, I finally came to at the sight of the train station: 'Anna, I'm going to have to run now, and I think it'll be easier if I do it without talking to you at the same time.' She agreed: 'Okay, call me back after!'

I ran through the station with the old green leather bag my mother had given me, which I think is cool but cuts into my neck. I didn't know it, but my train was running over the tracks at the same speed as me. On the platform, there was no train and my neck was bent like a croissant. I was out of breath and out of hope. After checking that I didn't recognise anyone around me, I burst into tears. My face crumpled like a crushed drinks can. I groaned. A woman from SNCF, so tall that people must point it out to her every day, came up to me and put her hand on my arm, asking what was wrong. I replied that my holidays were ruined, quite simply. That the very idea of going back to my shut-up apartment was unbearable. She seemed to be thinking: *Okay, First World problems*. But with professionalism, she gave me a compassionate look and offered to help me change my ticket on the yellow machine. I followed her, grateful, but when she dispassionately suggested a new train time I started crying again. I had realised that, despite her height and her SNCF badge, she had her own limits. Defeatedly, I told her that these other trains she was suggesting would mean I'd miss my connection. She said, as if I should be in a nursing home eating chicory, 'Don't say that, madame, no need to be pessimistic.' I thought that was stupid. She touched my arm again, but this time I didn't like it. On the inside I was regretting having met her. She handed me a warm ticket, brand new, and I took it from her with an ambivalent 'Thanks so much'. My oversized coat and sweater were letting in the departure hall air. I was cold. I was in the kind of situation where things aren't that bad really, but you feel like shutting down entirely all the same.

It was Gare Montparnasse, a few months before Louët. It was the moment when I decided to quit journalism. Inside the station, there was a shopping section with bakeries, macaron stands, a little Fnac and clothes shops. Rather than calling Anna back, I took refuge in the Levi's changing room and tried on jeans, yanking on each pair with violence. Thanks to this sadistic activity, the departure time of the new train came around quickly. I folded the jeans back up nicely. Once in Bordeaux, I did miss my connecting train as predicted, but I didn't cry this time. I even started to laugh instead. I called Daniel, with the kids on speaker, and said: 'Forgive me, I've missed my train because Anna acted like a GPS and I acted like someone from the nineties without the technological know-how to turn her off.' At the desk of the Bordeaux Ibis, there wasn't a young leading man like you usually see in this sort of hotel but a moustached seventy-year-old straight out of a sleazy motel. The man gave me a room with no chairs (two positions: standing up or lying down) which was just as glacial as the whole day had been. I slept with my clothes on, which would have disgusted Daniel, who, obsessive as he is, wishes I would wash twice a day. I should have called him. That would have given me a laugh: 'Hey, guess what? I'm sleeping with my clothes on.' (But I decided against it, struck by a memory. At the start of our relationship, I'd asked him how the Beatles song 'Girl' starts, and he started singing it from memory, in his high-pitched voice, twirling in the street. The most beautiful and least virile thing I've ever seen in my life.)

In the middle of the night, the cover slipped off my frozen shoulder. The deeper layers of my epidermis burst like bubble wrap. I wanted to sew the duvet to the edge of my neck. In the end I found the thermostat in the bathroom, a little white box with simple controls, one arrow pointing up and the other down. I pressed the up button so much that my throat dried out completely in seven minutes. My oesophageal mucus took on the consistency of a bath towel left for years at the bottom of a garden. That's the state I was in. From out in the Bordeaux night, the light from my bedroom would have formed a distinct square. A yellow ice cube. My throat hurt.

Opposite the king-size bed, a big mirror reflected the face of the black woman in a headwrap that hung on the wall behind me. Sitting on the bed, the top of my head covered the bottom of her chin. Her sombre, weary gaze was directed at me. She was urging me to talk. With her, I took stock of the situation with my friend. *What kind of mental force does Anna use to direct me around Paris? When did she become my boss? What's the link between my fear of displeasing her and my anxious child syndrome (which goes hand in hand with a submission to paternal authority)?* Omniscient Anna. That's what I named her that evening. *Omniscient Anna, I'm going to take the Métro at Gambetta because some things are easier when you make up your mind yourself.*

I described my friend's charms to my room-mate with the headwrap. Her beauty and her intelligence. My tendency to submit to her. I wrote in my phone notes: *Anna's geyser-like anger or the idea that I worry, I don't know.* I told the woman, 'Anna needs to be drip-fed with the correct reactions, incessantly. With information that suits her point of view. It's too much work. I quit!' That night I dreamed I was introducing Anna to some important people that she was going to climb Mont Blanc with. I was looking for them in the local swimming pool (quite off the mark, then); their number included Emmanuel Carrère, Elton John and Lacan. I don't endorse this mono-gendered selection from my unconscious. I can't do anything about that. In the dream, Anna called me to tell me she'd just had a 'delicious moment' with Lacan on top of a pink mountain and I congratulated her. Why couldn't I manage to say something as simple as: 'You could have waited for me, I'd have quite liked to be friends with Lacan too'? Shit, anyway, thanks to her, I was freezing to death. Or perhaps I only had myself to blame.

8

The Antelope Strategy

At 7 p.m., we were still sipping Martini. The conversation had unravelled: Rim and Anna were discussing, without much conviction, the pro-nuclear figure Jean-Marc Jancovici. Focused on the strength of the wind, I wasn't listening. It seemed like a dam in the sky had broken and gusts from beyond this world were plunging down into the bay. In the space of a few seconds, the sea had gone from very calm to all worked up. The island was going to drift off towards England. So that's why the seagulls didn't move earlier, I thought. They don't want to wind up eating fish and chip scraps out of the bins of London. I suggested we go back and take shelter inside the house, but Anna refused to leave the spectacular view. She latched on to a sort of big menhir and we copied her. Sheltering behind that big round rock, I reflected that the weekend was going better than expected. Our drinks hour was going okay, almost nicely, and this storm would engrave it in our memories. We passed five minutes like that, contemplating the foamy sea. Then Rim turned to me, pulled the hood of her yellow oilskin over her damp hair, tugged on the strings and closed her eyes as she asked me how far along I was with my feature-length. Not sure I'd heard correctly, I asked her to repeat herself.

'How are you getting on with your film?'

Hmm. I'd been consciously avoiding the subject ever since I'd started work on it. Firstly, because I still wasn't entirely sure what I was making. To work out if that was normal, I'd looked into the processes of some real artists. Unlike the composer Ravel, known for his extensive preparatory phases, and contrary to Shakespeare, who, it is said, thought long and hard before writing a single word, I was improvising. I told Rim that, and also, like I was speaking at an arts festival, that I didn't know if I would say that the quality of a production really depends on a better capacity for planning. I quoted the novelist E. L. Doctorow: 'Writing is like driving at night in the fog. You can only see as far as your headlights, but you can make the whole trip that way.' Laurent Mauvignier, who I'd have bet would be the king of the three-part plan, maintained that he let himself be carried away by the excrescences in his books. That they were even what pushed the text towards its own truth. Bertrand Blier thought that the secret to writing was to write quickly, to find an energy and a sincerity: the manuscript had to spring up like a poisonous mushroom. So that was it; I was, modestly, joining the improvisers. Since I was just starting out in film-making, I was trying to control a flow of thought that was close to a waking dream. I expelled it and then sculpted it clumsily. I put down bits of floor in front of the characters as they went along. It was precarious and difficult. All I knew was this: only the subject, its necessity, counted. Not for the art, but for the artist, so they wouldn't abandon the project halfway through. For their interior motor to rev, the concept had to take on the utmost importance, on the level of the survival of the species – yes, I said that. They nodded along kindly, but it was risky.

Anna asked: 'What is your subject?'

I pretended not to hear and poured myself another glass. Like an old Yale professor, I carried on: I'd recently begun to understand that it was the writing that had separated us, that it was one of the key reasons for the distance that had come between us. Each of us was digging her own distinct hole and motherhood had ceased to define us. Lately, the pursuit of our own interests, our own lives, had turned us into ice floes. I made a gesture with my hands of ice floes gently drifting apart on the Arctic Ocean. I knew that I called them less often because of my film-making, and some serious things were going unsaid. Maybe they'd even spoken about it between themselves? I was wallowing in solitude and secrecy, with a certain indulgence. I also admitted that there was a funny contradiction in how a work destined to be made public spends so long locked behind closed doors. But trying to explain an ongoing process, every attempt to answer the 'What's it about?' question, made me feel like I was talking nonsense. What we produce as grown adults always covers up something shameful. That's why I had such a hard time talking to them about it all, I concluded. That's why I was so absent and always lost in thought.

Anna seemed to understand, but Rim gave me a glassy look. She said: 'You haven't answered Anna's question. What is the subject?'

'Let me keep working on it,' I replied in a pleading tone. 'I'll tell you about it in the summer.'

'You could tell us about it and keep it vague,' Anna attempted.

'No, I'd rather not.'

Silence again; they were thinking. Would this conversation have a happy ending? No. Rim wouldn't take her eyes off me, waiting for me to go on.

'I'd have trouble carrying on if I could see in your eyes that you thought it was crap,' I added.

'No way – you're a genius, of course it's going to be interesting,' Anna said automatically.

'I wouldn't go that far,' Rim retorted.

She was cracking. Something wasn't right. The line of her mouth was broken. Emotion had given her skin a damp look. A strange and worrying thing: her cheeks were swelling. This had only happened twice before in the history of our friendship. The last time, a year earlier, was when I'd told her that, given her age, I didn't understand why she was still so angry with her mother. It was a provocation, said to piss her off. I'd drunk two pints of beer and for once decided to take the side of everyone who finds Emmanuelle adorable and charming, because they've never witnessed anything else. But I'm fully aware of the situation behind closed doors: I know that this woman, who lacked essential attention in childhood, knows only how to charm or destroy, nothing else, and disparages anything that makes her feel insecure. She sullies, trashes and twists the honest intentions of anyone who doesn't bow down to her. She exteriorises her depression, smothers her enemies with it. But under the patio heater on the terrace, Rim was annoying me with the never-ending topic of her parents and the evening was becoming a drag. 'Come on, we're adults now, let's stop crying over other people's psyches,' I'd said. I'd added that her mother had always been nice to me – and the 'always' was false and the 'to me' showed the extent of the problem.

From Rim's point of view, what I'd said next was surely the worst of betrayals. 'You do exaggerate about your mother.' The absolute denial, from the most steadfast witness of her life, of all that she'd managed to put together in the last few years. It was really low because you never know if you're right on your own. When it comes to yourself, you're suspicious of everything. So if the people who are supposed to understand you frown and say that the boat from your childhood wasn't yellow, not at all, but actually red, who are you supposed to believe? Her cheeks swelled up, she invented a meeting and ran off.

Swollen cheeks too, years and years ago, on the day I told her what I thought of her university boyfriend, the guy she spent three years with and who came from the same wealthy background we'd grown up in. Stanislas was as rich as his three hundred friends. In the first months of their relationship, I'd seen Rim happy to belong to a social group that had the financial heft of an entire country. The boy, who lived right by the Jardin d'Acclimatation, threw parties on the porch of his Basque-inspired house. His mother, who worked in fashion, gave Rim clothes: a Burberry raincoat, a Chanel dress. Other than by her face, I didn't recognise her any more. She looked like the best-dressed girls from our childhood. Béatrice Dalle Middleton. It was almost a nightmare. Rim and Stanislas were the first French couple to own a projector. Every Saturday evening, the same text from Rim: *Come watch a film on the projector!* It was unbearable. You could tell from my face that I found it unbearable. For Rim, my expression had become tiring, and for me, the worst part wasn't that she had changed, but that the fact of her having changed was never acknowledged in any way, while I would have liked to start each of our conversations with that preamble. Then the rest would have been tolerable.

The heart of the problem was that I didn't like Stanislas, a carbon footprint record holder who never went a week without at least a medium-haul flight. His favourite words: *sunset*, *playa*, *kids* and *besos*. He worked for his father, who he was in love with (we should be able to make a ruthless judgement of the first idealised figure regardless of gender. Everyone gives mothers a hard time). Stanislas worked for the company his father had founded, a manufacturer of private jets. His vocation was to become the number two, then the number one. When he spoke to his father on the phone at 9 p.m., Stan would tell him everything he'd heard around the office. Total allegiance. Under the paternal thumb, like Alfredo in *La traviata*. But if a son submits to that first rule, what won't he submit to? Nothing makes me sadder.

After a year and a half, it became clear that Rim didn't like him any more either; you could tell because she started wearing tinted glasses like an insomniac. Kate Middleton in rehab. One Sunday afternoon, having lunch near my old place in Belleville, she drank three spritzes in a row. Unable to hold back, I told her to break up with the guy since it couldn't be said that he did her any good. I used that convoluted phrasing, 'It can't be said that he does you any good,' like in *A Simple Summer's Day* by Frédéric Berthet, when the narrator replies 'You could not be mistaken' to the baker asking if he'd like a baguette. And even though I should have left it at that – I already seemed like the sanctimonious cousin with a medal round her neck, worried when her parents drink strong liquor – I opened the floodgates. I said that Stan was ugly and lifeless. She tensed her jaw and closed her Vuitton bag. I carried on criticising him. Her cheeks swelled up. The restaurant door slammed. Walking along the street, even though I was entirely in the wrong, I managed to get angry with her too. I thought that she'd been imposing a sort of exhibitionism on me for months now. She would parade her unhappiness and then, having ended up traumatising me, return to her air-conditioned home cinema. We were performing a dance in which she played Pinocchio and I was Jiminy Cricket. How could we make it stop? She was cramping my style. We didn't laugh like we used to. I had to listen to the same mental slop incessantly. She would say: 'I don't love him any more. I'm going to leave him.' Then: 'I can't live without him, that would tear me apart.'

'Come on, Rim, you're contradicting yourself. Get a grip. I'm used to more mental fortitude from you than this.'

After that lunch, we'd burned our bridges, which given my youth and confidence didn't take much for me. I was sure that we'd reunite eventually, and a year later, once we were done with university, we did indeed. I called her after stumbling upon an animal encyclopedia in a bookshop in the Marais. This book made me realise that with Rim I'd practised something they called the 'antelope strategy'. Antelopes run together until they realise that their togetherness puts them in danger, it said, and then they separate. To start with, fleeing collectively improves the chances of escape because a single animal can't deflect attention from itself. But once the predator gets its claws into the group, the prey scatters and it's each beast for themselves. My friend's name ('antelope' in Arabic) became entwined in what I was reading. The entry and its yellowed images were speaking to me personally. Telling me off. *Three spritzes, a projector and you left her to the lions?* I closed the book and dialled her number: 'Hey Rim, remember me?' On the phone, I told her I'd been a bad friend ('You were sinking and I stepped aside') and she told me she was single ('You were right, I broke up with him and I kept the projector'). Afterwards, she didn't ever have a go at me about it. She had, it seemed, given me a second chance.

An observation here: we often give friendship a superior status to romantic love. But in reality, when a friend isn't doing well they're abandoned more quickly because there are no social structures in place to support the relationship.

While a spool of tightly wound wire keeps couples together – friends in common, children, the house – there's nothing like that for friendship. And how can you put up with the conversations on loop, the crazed eyes, the chain-smoking and the chain of problems when there's nothing forcing you to? How can you put up with changing styles and values? Who wants to become the owner of a Labrador with big wet eyes who can talk and calls you every day to tell you they haven't followed any of your advice? Seriously, who? Other than a total martyr. Or a better person than me.

9

The Film

Rim hates conflict. In general, when she's pissed off, she limits herself to making euphemisms that only she understands. But this time was going to be different. Although the sun had disappeared into the water, I could see an untold quantity of sharp words bristling behind her gappy teeth. Okay, it's time, I thought. It's finally going to come out. At this point, I was still curious.

'I know what your film is about,' she said.

'What do you mean?'

'I went looking for my cigarettes in your bedroom earlier. There were ten pages out on your bed.'

'Your cigarettes in my bedroom? And you sat down and read it?'

'Yeah, that's right, I read it.'

'You felt you had the right to do that?'

'Absolutely. But if you must know, I did set myself a moral boundary. I didn't move anything. And I didn't go looking for the rest of it.'

'Congratulations. And did you like it?'

'Honestly, it wasn't terrible.'

'I'm sorry.'

'No problem, I'm sure you'll find your audience. But tell me, Armelle, at what point were you planning to disclose that it was about us?'

'Listen, that's good timing, because I was planning to tell you right now. Too bad, isn't it, that you missed a chance to behave nicely.'

I wavered over whether to continue with this ironic tone and accusations of privacy violations. It was a line of defence that wouldn't work very well because the lack of respect for privacy was, let's be honest, coming from my side. The main character of my script was, as a matter of fact, largely inspired by Rim. Like how in a greengrocer's you pick up whatever catches your eye, I'd plucked her personality traits here and there and, after this psycho-logical shopping spree, had even gone so far as to conjure up a childhood trauma to explain the incoherence of her behaviour. Her refusal to be touched and her paradoxical orgies. Her dissociation between the party girl who takes annual leave for her birthday versus the Gestapo officer who has to be in charge of everything. Her sportiness and the cigarettes she sometimes chain-smokes. Her talent ver-sus what she herself calls her professional underachieve-ment. I had completely fabricated a rape at the sports cen-tre in Neuilly-sur-Seine. At the end of the film, the 'Rimian' character tells this secret to her closest friend, a clone of Anna. The revelation takes place in the rain, outside Bichat hospital, where my mother had been a patient in real life after the fire in Belleville... A strange cocktail, for Rim, of biographical reference points shaken in a liquid of fiction. And judging by Anna's expression, it would be a total mindfuck for her to read too. I'd also fed off the real-life tensions that existed between Rim and Anna, Rim and me, Anna and me; I'd pulled at their threads again and again to create the drama. I didn't know how much Rim had read, but I knew she was good at pick-up sticks and everything that required fine motor skills. She'd understood that I'd juggled with our lives. My mind went blank. Actually, no, that's not entirely true: I thanked Heaven that Anna hadn't found the text instead. I thought I could still wriggle out of it.

'It's fiction, Rim.'

'Ah, yeah, of course. With Ava Gardner in the starring role, right?'

'The character you're talking about isn't you.'

'But I'm not the one you have to tell that to, Armelle! You need to tell yourself. Because if you think you've captured me, you're completely wrong... If that's me, it's me massacred on the piano.'

Because the wind was blowing ever stronger, her voice progressively increased in volume. I thought: Yes, or it's you as told by a compulsive liar. You caught in an incomprehensible dream where you'd suddenly turn into my mother. I replied: 'No, it's not a massacre. Or an assassination. It's a mix of my subjective idea of you and my narrative objective. It's a film, I can't say everything.'

'Oh, are you hearing yourself, you stupid bitch?'

Without rising to the insult, I carried on: 'Autofiction is experience seen through a kaleidoscope so everything gets distorted. It's nothing to do with reality. It's a story with little bits of my life inside, but it's a story first and foremost.'

'I couldn't care less about your attempts at patchwork. I don't give a fuck! It seems like the little bits of your life that you're talking about are actually my life.'

Her grey eyes shot flames and I saw her consider throwing her glass of Martini in my face. I thought that the tension was perhaps not going to ease from this point, and that the questions she'd ask me would be more and more demanding. On my side, I was drowning in questions to myself: Why did I bring my script with me in the first place? Did I have the subconscious aim of drawing inspiration from this trip to use in my screenplay? Of course I did, it was obvious. Keen ear during the day and scribe at night, that was the unspoken plan. I'd wanted to transcribe whole sections of dialogue between us rather than having to invent them. I was realising now that it was even the reason I'd said yes to this weekend. But why did I leave those pages on my bed, only a few steps away from theirs? Did I want to be read, did I want the drama? Could a Freudian slip be any more blatant?

'What I mean is, it's you seen through several filters. Which means you can distance yourself from it.'

'Fucking hell, stop with the teacher voice. Take me out of the film, Armelle, and go and buy yourself some Play-Doh instead.'

'Oh, why are you being such a pain in the arse about it, Rim, what harm can it do you? Your name isn't in there, no secrets, no shame, there's nothing. Just a magnifying effect, that's all.'

'It's theft. And I haven't been raped.'

'Obviously you haven't been raped. That's exactly the proof that it's not you! And by the way, it's not me either. The *I* is another. You can see that. I'm not at all the terrible neurotic I make myself out to be in the film!'

'Well, sorry, but yes you are. I recognised you very well. Try to understand what you're doing. You're taking hold of me, you describe me as you see me, however you want – badly, that is – you change the colour of my hair, you add in a rape to justify the inconsistencies in my character and after all that you're content, you think it's art? No, it's just a shitty spider's web, nothing else.'

'Come on, Rim, stop, you're being unfair. You're being nasty. It's a work of art. I'm parodying us, you're not identifiable, whereas I'm exposing myself. It's only me who's compromised there.'

'So when should I go and see myself be raped in the cinema?'

'Not you, an actor.'

'Go fuck yourself, Armelle.'

Of course I should have gone and fucked myself. It was, if anything, well overdue that I go fuck myself. The last few weeks, as I'd worked, I couldn't deny that ethical questions had been falling on me like chunks of ice sliding off a roof in the morning. I'd even read Elias Canetti's memoirs, to see what he had written about Iris Murdoch, who had taken inspiration from her affair with him in one of her novels (*The Flight from the Enchanter*). Was he upset with her for it? Well, I should have noted that yes he was, very. Enormously, even. His contempt for her quality as a writer depressed me ('She listened like a deaf person who has to pay extra attention to understand the least thing'), as did his indelicacy towards her ('I barely noticed when I penetrated her and she didn't seem to notice either'). After that, I went looking for advice from American screenwriters who describe the way they create 'composite characters' by putting their various friends in kitchen blenders together. And in preparation for this fight, which I'd anticipated in my head many times, I'd even tried to learn off by heart the list of models Proust had used for Charlus in *In Search of Lost Time*, but I could only remember two: Robert de Montesquiou and Aimery de La Rochefoucauld.

In the weeks leading up to Louët, I'd been falling asleep with moral dilemmas that took the shape of my pillow: How much of a person can you capture without them getting upset? Is it better to commit a thousand tiny thefts or to seize hold of a big chunk of personality and drown it in a pool of untrue details? Can you write without hurting anyone? How can you capture the truth without trotting out the same old clichés? Would a purely imaginative work of fiction be of any interest at all? How can you proceed so that it would be impossible afterwards – for other people as much as for yourself – to trace the tracks laid by reality into fiction?

One night, I arrived at the conclusion that we have the right to make use of the memories that exist in the closed space of a relationship, but not anything that goes outside of it and into the public domain, or that would allow identification by other people. However, I was aware that the inverse could be just as easily defended, since what was only known to two people was exactly what constituted the pact of friendship. Clearly I'd fucked up.

'I'm sorry, Rim. I understand it must be unpleasant to read. But believe me, it wasn't done against you. I don't wish you any ill.'

That was true, and at that point I still thought that quarter of an hour later I would be back in my yellow bedroom, where I'd hide those ten pages and the rest of the script under a pile of clothes while Rim and Anna would go back to their blue room, still in a bit of a mood with me but nothing too serious in the end, nothing that would last until the next day, when suddenly, though I'd forgotten she existed, which never happens, Anna jumped into the conversation.

'What about me? Am I in it?'

'Go and look, it's in Armelle's room, help yourself,' said Rim.

'No, don't go,' I said.

'Well, am I in it or not?'

(What should I say? Did she want to be in it? Of course she did – when it's hypothetical, everyone dreams of being a source of inspiration; it lends weight to your being, it's flattering, remarkable, it elevates you above the masses. In reality, though, it's only tolerable when the person involved has

217

defined the terms themselves. The only acceptable way: a shower of glitter with the glitter checked and pre-approved. For fuck's sake, no one was in it. Or rather yes, everyone was, but no one was identifiable. Be careful now.)

'No, you're not in it, Anna.'

'Well, just a bit,' said Rim. 'It's a mix of you and her narrative objective. All that in the national film archive, for eternity.'

'Stop it, she's not in it at all.'

'There's a girl who looks like her though!'

'That's me!'

'Ah, that's enough, you're talking shit now.'

'Be quiet, Rim. Sort out your problems with me without shit-stirring, please.'

'The shit's already there, Armelle. And I'm no expert, but I don't think Rim's the one doing the stirring,' said Anna, getting up. Once standing, she added: 'I don't understand the problem. Does it make us look bad, is that it?'

'No. Ambiguous.'

'You'll have to excuse me, I'm going to read this right now.'

'It's a declaration of love,' I said.

And she took three steps.

10

It's Really Come to This

I threw myself forwards to stop Anna. I grabbed her by the sleeve of her oilskin. 'Don't move,' I cried. Anna didn't fight back because she doesn't lower herself to that sort of thing. I was holding her wrist with both hands and Rim was staring me down like the buffalo she can become. How to calm down my oldest friend? I began talking very quickly. Pathetically, I heard myself repeating that my manuscript showed her in a positive light, that my producer had even said that the character inspired by her was his favourite, 'a strong character', he'd said, and anyway, *what was I saying, she makes me lose my head*, you couldn't even call it inspiration, it wasn't about that. My breathing: getting shorter and shorter. The character was born beyond the true or false. She, Rim, was maybe one of the sources of her existence, like a distant ancestor, but that was all. She would have to see the film with a clear head to understand. Or in ten years' time, to have more detachment and clemency towards it. In reality, between my characters and my friends, 'any resemblance was purely coincidental', as the credits would make clear.

It was also my freedom of expression, I said boldly. I could understand, of course, that it would be difficult for Rim. To feel manipulated by someone else's words, pushed without a second thought through a funhouse mirror to land, your nose where your cheek should be, on a film reel that's halfway through playing your verbal tics. But that's what you get if you hang out with anxious laptop-tappers, and anyway, you had to keep things in perspective; there were serious problems, and then there was this. They knew me well, what exactly had they expected? Anna had even talked about it this morning; I'd heard her when I was in the kitchen. Becoming my characters was maybe even what they'd been hoping for deep down, ever since my short film had come out. Friendship is a tangle of perspectives, and this film's aim was only to show mine. Not accepting that would be akin to totalitarianism. A screenplay bore no stamp of eternal truth. It would be forgotten in two years, lost entirely in two centuries. And in the meantime, all it would be was a testament to a period of time, a tiny piece of folklore. It was hardly a matter of life or death. And then I reiterated that anything that belonged to them alone had been left untouched. I'd only made use of what was shared among us, the energies that circulated between us, because there was no part of life that was mine alone. 'Everything is shared, Rim. It's like memory. Without communication, it doesn't exist,' I said. Contradicting myself even further, I asked Rim – staring at her intensely to underline the seriousness of the question – if she wanted me to add certain qualities to her character or take out hurtful details: 'Are there bits of dialogue that you don't like?' Without waiting for her to reply, I finished off with a long-winded speech on how there's no such thing as an exact portrait. All that could come out of a film were impressionist contours, silhouettes that the viewers would each see in their own ways, diluting the truth of the original models even further. It should be simply taken as an homage: for example, the character based on Rim always fell asleep to Debussy's 'Clair de lune', and that was one of the loveliest things she used to do as a teenager, smoking joints in bed. I loved that Rim listened to classical music not to impress me but to calm herself down.

It was right then, when I started to wax lyrical about Debussy, that Rim's anger exploded. Forget Debussy – this was a Wagnerian fury. My friend rushed at me, grabbed and pulled my arm behind my back, saying: 'Don't you give a fuck about hurting people?' I managed to hold on to Anna's wrist and even squeezed tighter, knowing I was hurting her. Wincing, Anna asked: 'Has it really come to this?'

Yes, we were in a full-on wrestling match. I stamped on Rim's foot. She yelled: 'Oh my God, you're totally crazy! If you don't let Anna go right now I'm going to bring your script down here. Anyway, what did you think was going to happen? We were going to see your shitty film in the cinema eventually!'

Then Rim swallowed her saliva and changed tack. She let go of my arm. She started to pull on my coat as hard as she could instead. I was dragged away from Anna and was losing my balance.

So I pushed her to get her off me.

What was most important to me in that moment was that Anna, whose opinion counted so much to me, didn't move a millimetre. That she didn't get to the script. I didn't want her to read it and think less of me. Not now, not here, on this island that we could only escape by swimming. At another time, maybe, after the screenplay had been cleaned up, signed off on and produced. When I'd have found the vocabulary to discuss it. But since none of that had happened yet, I pushed Rim harder than intended.

With a rage I can't explain.

Where did it come from?

Maybe from her status as the oldest.

From when she had said to me, before a dance class, that I lacked grace. From her telling me, every day of my childhood, that I was rubbish at piano.

From my fear, since she was gearing up to flatten me herself.

From the malice in her look, that look that had always held me back from doing what I wanted, even though I felt like I'd spent my whole life appeasing her so she'd continue to protect me. (Wanting to make her happy – sure. But in the end, all I was allowed was a half-life, in a corner, so I wouldn't bother anyone.)

From my lack of words, since Anna's presence stopped me from talking to her about the film as I would have liked to.

From my brain coming unstuck.

Without cliff edges, life would be gentler.

I didn't understand straight away what had happened,

but although her body should have hit the menhir behind her and come back towards me in a rebound effect, instead it veered strangely to the right, towards the edge of the cliff. She only just kept her balance, her knees bent, and I'd never seen so much uncertainty on anyone's face. A little over a foot behind her, there was emptiness. One big step. I was afraid. If the cross and the edge of the rock formed a line from A to B, she was at point B. Which disappeared. Her body disappeared.

Whoosh.

She let out a scream.

Sky before me. No friend, only sky.

I yelled her name.

My vision clouded over in fear.

The landscape shattered like glass.

I turned towards Anna, who I'd let go of to push Rim. She was stock-still and staring over the horizon, which reassured me. If she wasn't looking for her in the dark water, it must be because she wasn't down there. Anna was intelligent, and had seen everything. Then I realised that she had simply disassociated and her eyes weren't responding any more. I panicked. I uttered words that didn't belong to me. In an authoritative voice, like a ship's captain had possessed my body, I said that the wind was blowing at over sixty-four knots and that we needed to act fast before the ocean swept Rim away. I murmured to Anna: 'Look for her, just please go and look for her.' I felt myself falling into a kind of madness. I picked up a big stone and threw it into the sea as if that could bring my friend back in a sort of reverse physical movement: *Bam, yes, here I am*. I noted that Anna was still totally immobile, even though she should have taken charge of the situation. That was her role. I shouted, 'Rim!'

Rim didn't appear.

I said out loud that everything would be all right.

Because Rim had muscles and she knew how to use them.

I sat down and cried, the wind flattening my ears. Anna came to life.

'We have to call the authorities. Even if we don't know where she is.'

'Yes,' I said.

I heard her oilskin rustling behind me as she started to run. I stood up and, finally, dared to go over to where the ground fell away. And there I saw her. I saw Rim.

11

Resignation

Rim's fall had been broken by a protrusion in the cliff. Her legs were on this jutting rock; her feet seemed driven into it. She was on her front, the rest of her body arched against the cliff face. Her hair, her back, her thighs were visible. Rim looked like she was having an upside-down nap in a stone hammock, halfway down to the sea. She had slid down the cliff face, and as she'd hurtled down the rock wall her arm must have hit an obstacle, because it was bloody. She hadn't fallen too far. Then she tilted her head towards me; her face looked completely absent.

Behind me, I heard Anna's creaking coat and panicked panting as she came back. Motionless at the edge of the cliff, next to me, she followed my gaze and saw her too. Her shoulders slumped. She smiled. 'Good fucking heavens above,' she said. Then she shouted to Rim that the emergency services were coming, that they were already on their way.

'Thank you,' I said to Anna, squeezing her shoulder. 'It's okay. She's safe for now.'

'Yes, but we're still going to have to go and get her.'

Anna got down via a steep, narrow path I hadn't spotted on the side of the cliff. It didn't take long: within two minutes, she'd hooked her arms under Rim's armpits and gently lifted her up. The wind made the whole operation tricky; the protrusion in the cliff face was about the size of two Parisian balconies, and Anna had trouble keeping her balance. Nonetheless, she carried her, lifted her, supported her, dragged her along the path and managed, by alternating all these actions many times, to bring her back up to where I was. Anna lay Rim at the foot of the 1841 cross. The tear in the clothing at her right elbow was shaped like a flower in bloom. The stone underneath her ruined arm turned red. My friend's mouth was trembling, the little scar on her top lip quivering, her cat eyes turned towards me again but looking off into the distance, towards the Taureau. Rim didn't seem fully conscious. Anna asked me to keep her arm elevated and not to touch anything else while she went to get something to cover her with, along with the life jackets for our return to the mainland. I got the message: don't try anything, I'd already done enough as it was. In her absence, there was nothing to distract me from my guilt. I held my friend's arm firmly and murmured 'Sorry' over and over, without getting the slightest reaction. The strange feeling you get when you leave an island, like when you leave the ground, was coupled with the feeling that the land waiting for me on the other side had changed entirely.

I heard the sound of a speedboat getting clearer and clearer.

Thanks to Anna, the emergency team was already there. Thanks to her it had arrived in less than quarter of an hour (eight minutes for an ambulance in Paris). I realised that we'd made a huge fuss about being on a desert island, when in fact the distance separating it from the mainland was laughable. The black cable bringing electricity here no longer resembled an intestinal beast but a simple pipe.

A huge woman, her hair as red as mine, was driving the boat. She was my XXL version, with boat-steering skills. She moored up. Two young men in overalls, who looked like they might be her younger brothers, got out with an orange stretcher and a big box of equipment and ran towards us. I've forgotten what happened next. All I remember is Rim lying on the floor of the boat, her eyes closed and her cheeks splashed by the waves. The wind had dropped. The sea calmed.

My memory returns later, near a big roaring fireplace. In the crêperie in Morlaix, Anna ordered two sweet crêpes one on top of the other, and I nothing. My friend spent the meal trying to reassure me: Rim wasn't dead, for one thing. Then, that the accident was down to a series of circumstances. The conversation had turned ugly and we'd made sudden movements. Anna didn't mention my screenplay. The word was forbidden, and I was grateful to her for it. I had pushed Rim in self-defence because she was pulling me towards her, that was all. The wind and the instability of the cliff had done the rest. Being in the wrong place at the wrong time: it was karma. 'It's as senseless as when people get crushed in a crowd,' she told me, kindly. 'Yes, I see,' I responded, remembering the strength of my movement. As I wasn't talking much, in the end Anna got out her iPhone. After some googling, she found out that the 1841 cross honoured a walker, the victim of a rockslide while he was quietly reading his book. 'So it was basically the first grave in the island cemetery,' I said without laughing. As we left the restaurant, I thought back to how seriously Rim had taken the risk of rockslides on Louët. I had flashbacks of our morning coffee, the signs forbidding us to climb to the top of the island, the star that had glittered on her neck. A lucky star, I'd hoped naively.

'You're shaking,' said Anna as we got back to the hotel.

'Yeah, it's like convulsions. I don't know how to stop it.'

'Put your jumper on and take a deep breath and count to five.'

'That's nice of you, but no. I'm a monster. I don't want to count to five, it doesn't make any sense.'

In the two-star family hotel in Morlaix, we booked a basic room with two beds. Anna told me that she'd called Niels from the hospital. He would be arriving late morning the next day, and he'd asked us to go back to Paris; he'd rather look after Rim on his own. As we undressed, Anna and I only talked about logistical matters for the following day. What train, and what time to set the alarm. In contrast with the red sun that had illuminated our last night in Tunisia, all that came through the bedroom window was an insignificant, yellowish street light. On the way to her bed, Anna stopped next to me to take me in her arms. I allowed a brief embrace. I was in despair, but I no longer wanted to talk about it. Not to her nor to Daniel. Anna went out in the corridor to phone Panchi, to tell him that the girls' weekend was over, that she was coming home early. I heard her murmuring, answering yes or no. A quarter of an hour later, she came back into the room without any comforting words to pass along from Panchi. With nothing to say at all. She lay down on her mattress, turned off the little bedside lamp, pulled the covers over herself and fell asleep on her back. I kept my eyes open. I scrutinised her: *That's what an unchanged existence looks like.*

The outdated room had dark-pink walls. A Breton wardrobe took up half the space. On the garden side, a balcony looked out over trees that were nice and green and lush. The window was ajar. It was raining. Outside, it smelled of earth. In another life, I would have felt at ease, but in this one, it was a disaster. At midnight, I texted my therapist, who had retired to the Ardèche among her books, to ask if we could have a phone session, and she replied within a minute: *Of course, Armelle. I'm always here. Call me tomorrow, I hope it's nothing serious.* It was hard to say; nothing had ever been so serious. I was sure that this time, without her help, I was at risk of losing my mind or my senses from one minute to the next.

Later, the phone in the bedroom rang, a ringing, *driiiing*, from another time. I picked up before it woke Anna, and someone from the Morlaix hospital, who didn't give either their name or their rank, told me that Rim was out of danger. The haemorrhage had been stopped. Her humerus had been fractured in three places, so the doctors had inserted a metal orthopaedic rod all the way down her arm. They'd closed it up with stitches. Rim's body had taken the implant well and she had eaten. She would have it in there for two years, then the rod would be removed. I said, 'That's great, thank you, good news.' I hung up and gazed at the strong trees in the interior courtyard. An hour later, still unable to sleep, I wandered the hotel corridors, all upholstered in a thick fleur-de-lys-patterned carpet, which didn't make me laugh. I bumped into the manager, an older Breton woman with a small forehead. I told her about the day's horror, and she slipped me a bottle of sedatives. Behind her, a clock hung on the wall with twelve Bigouden headdresses in different colours to mark the hours. Back in my bed, I reflected that a person's beauty really does depend on the size of their forehead, always. I also admitted to myself that I wouldn't have the elegance required to kill myself with a bottle of pills. I replayed the scene over and over until daybreak, the way Rim's body had moved to the right, a thousand times. I wondered, with what I now consider some real nerve, if that strange sideways movement hadn't been a subconscious action on her part. Whether the rape scene in my screenplay hadn't touched on something real after all. Had she endangered herself because I'd guessed her trauma?

At breakfast the next day, I heard the older Breton woman telling her husband about us, calling us the lighthouse girls. That's what we were now: a news item.

On the train to Paris, as I wallowed in sadness, through half-closed eyes I saw Clémence and Louis go past with huge suitcases, clearly on their way to cross the Channel. They were already speaking English and wearing Oxford sweatshirts under their big beige macs. I would have swapped lives with them in an instant. Anna had seen them too, but she didn't say anything. She was managing to read the book reviews in *Le Monde*.

After we got back from Louët, I went to spend a solo week at my academic mother-in-law's house in Beauce, where I spent my time screening Daniel's calls, taking glum trips to Super U and thinking about the physical principle of a fall, the force of gravity, which isn't supposed to pull people to the right. I hoped our Tunisian WhatsApp group would be revived, but the notifications never arrived. My phone screen seemed frozen. Nothing happened on it. I suspected it wasn't turned on properly. I shook it. I called my mother, she picked up; it was working. During that stay, I realised that Niels had unfriended me on Facebook and that Rim's profile had disappeared altogether. That evening, I wondered if I hadn't dreamed the call from the hospital. I could no longer guarantee a hundred per cent that that ring from another century had resounded in the room. Had Rim pulled through?

When I got back to Paris, I sent a letter to *Arts* to confirm my resignation. On the day my contract ended, I wrote to Anna to tell her that our ten years of journalism spent side by side were over and asked her to put my things to one side. I didn't have the strength to go back there and see people I'd have to explain Rim's fall to. Never mind the leaving drinks. Anna replied that I could count on her. She said she thought back fondly to Burgundy, our first assignment together and our evening at the service station, and she wished me a good IMDb page, if that was still a thing.

12

The Sound of Silence

Outside of my work, I don't speak to anyone any more. Or no one speaks to me any more; it's unclear. It's been that way for the last three and a half years. My social life is like a negative integer. I pretend I'm okay, but Daniel knows the truth. The guilt eats away at me. The father of my children thinks that I should be on medication for my ongoing depression, and he's getting impatient – I was fun before, how long is he going to have to put up with this, etc. He insists on pills, but I'm resistant. The idea of getting rid of my guilt makes me feel guilty. I pull the wool over the boys' eyes, but when I have dinner with them, I always end up opening my sketchbook and drawing empty shapes after a while. Sometimes I manage to make jokes. I wake them up at the weekend by singing 'A Whole New World' from *Aladdin* like I did when they were little, that's one joke. I eat tins of Petit Navire tuna for every meal.

I put the screenplay right at the bottom of the Dr Martens box, underneath my childhood photos. This means I sleep on top of it. This abandoned script is the most important document of my life. I love it and I hate it. I still write screenplays, but nothing grandiose or personal – fictional stories that tackle societal problems (the end of life, or addiction). I struggle to obtain writing grants, like all the screenwriters in my shared workspace in the Oberkampf neighbourhood. Often, I imagine that Rim has gone to live in Oslo. That's what I would have done if I were her. So I've put Oslo in the first slot in my weather app. When I'm on the rammed Métro on my way home, I sometimes also end up imagining her living in a little wooden cabin on the edge of a lake, next to Ludwig Wittgenstein's Norwegian chalet. I reread the Austrian philosopher, who doesn't draw an obvious link between will and action, something which suits me. An arm can raise itself, out of reflex (in class, for example). And I extrapolate: an arm can push, out of distress.

What's left of the fact that I pushed Rim if we subtract the fact that I pushed Rim? An intention, or an emptiness?

Last month, I ran into Anna outside the Théâtre du Châtelet. I almost looked away but, at the last second, I thought that was stupid and I looked her right in the eyes. After some awkward small talk – how are you; all right, and you; yeah, not too bad – Anna told me she often thought about our trip to Tunisia, and I lied when I replied 'Me too'. Then I asked her if she remembered that, on our last evening in Djerba, it was her who had advised me to write a film about friendship.

'I have no recollection of that at all. But what are you trying to say? That I'm responsible for the accident?'

'No.'

'That's just as well, because no one's giving you orders, Armelle, you do things all by yourself!'

'It's more complicated than that, but yes.'

'You should take responsibility for your actions.'

'For the screenplay or the fall?'

'Both.'

'I feel both responsible and not responsible.'

'You are responsible. Your tongue is a blade. But we can still love you all the same.'

'What should I have done?'

'Trusted us. Let me go and find the script. Let us read it. I know you don't like those Care Bear sentiments. That you'll never cry "Long live sisterhood! Friendship between women is straightforward and magnificent!" I know simplistic ideas frustrate you and that you look for reverse angles everywhere. But through your snobbery, through your reasoning, through demanding your independence, you lose sight of what's important.'

'I miss you both.'

'My number hasn't changed.'

Anna left and, like Rim would have done, I started to hum 'The Sound of Silence' by Simon and Garfunkel, making my way back up the Rue de Rivoli. I went past the seashell cafe, turned my head so as not to see the leather booth on the inside, walked back to my house, and my mood plummeted.

Three years have flowed past since Louët, but Rim's birthday always falls on 23 May. These days now aren't days. Everything is fixed, nothing is flexible. My bed is made of cement. Daniel's scrambled eggs clog my throat. Today my hair is dry to the point of breaking, as if I were sitting in the middle of a forest fire. I leave the balcony, go back to bed, and to force the memories out I write Rim a letter on my phone.

Rim, time hasn't done anything, I still can't explain. If I pushed you, I think it's because I was in a double bind. Next to that cross, I got stuck in a crazy loop. If I let Anna go, she'll go and read the script. But if I hold her back, Rim will bring it to her. My action was an accident of thought. Nothing else comes to me. What fills my head is the loss.

Wherever you are, I want you to know that my life consists of whispering things to you. On my desk I've got a photo of us at my first proper party, the one you threw at your house. Our faces are perfect, our bodies the same height. My belt buckle is a metal star. You're wearing a headband and a stripy miniskirt. There weren't many people there, some kids had cancelled, but you said great, more room for us to dance.

Today it's your birthday, the parties are long gone, and I realise how much you protected me. Without your sturdiness, I would have ended up eating my ski mittens. I would have been lost in the sadness of my parents' relationship, the hopelessness in our apartment, the width of the boulevards and the rust-coloured corridor. And then I would have become an overwhelmed, vacant adult. I owe you my human form.

Your absence makes the world incomprehensible. It's as bewildering as if the mirror no longer showed my reflection. I'd like to have you back, just so you could stop me doing stupid things. A little plastic surgery, for example – it's tempting. But it would be idiotic. Do you remember that when we were nine, without your intervention I would have adopted a dolphin? And the dolphin would have died. And I would have cried. The stories we tell ourselves in life.

I think about your wrecked arm and my elbow that itches on rainy days. They communicate. Even if you don't love me any more, you're still my genesis, the proof of my own lifespan. I would have liked to have been the same thing for you, for my face to show your age.

Since Louët, I've been a woman full of gaps. I've started to disappear. My eardrums miss your terrible singing. In front of places I associate with you, I go into slow motion and Daniel does too, matching my pace without realising.

I would have liked us to go back to the horse, when we're old, to do a naked rodeo. Imagine. The old Duke of Orléans, at his age, who knows what that might do to him sexually. You'd help me get up there. We'd be immortalised in black-and-white by a young photographer passing by, and be reproduced on an infinite number of postcards. The two of us, in every good corner shop in France. Not giving a fuck about anything, sharing the supreme consolation of growing old. Without you, what's left? The sun?

After the ride, we'd go and drink hot chocolate on Boulevard Saint-Germain. Our hair thinning a little, lips covered in whipped cream, our papery stomachs like twins, our shoulders lacking muscle but protected by gaudy purple faux-fur mantles. So there we would have been, two shrunken little bookends, giggling away.

Happy to have nothing else to be doing.

I miss you so much.

This 23 May, I faintly hear my sons laughing as they watch Mr Bean sketches, their latest obsession. Rim and I hold the world record for watching *Dirty Dancing*. Also *The Bodyguard* and *Grease*. *It's electrifying.*

I lost Rim. It's my fault. I don't know if it's a shame that friendship is like a free trade system and no one is obliged to see anyone, and therefore Rim is not obliged to see me. I shouldn't send her this letter, which is like a window display of my feelings, but I think it's time to emerge from this purgatory, this passivity. It's been three years and I don't know what I'm waiting for any more. Today, after having rewatched the film of our friendship, it occurs to me that if you shut yourself off from the world, like I've done, you'll inevitably fall apart. But now I want to see her.

I hate it when even an insignificant connection is broken. Losing Rim and Anna, to whom my past and sense of meaning belong – I can't bear it. If you imagine that the film of a person's life is made up of three superimposed reels, that these three reels give it its colour and depth, well, I'm missing two. Since Brittany, I've been living an achromatic life where happiness is the mere absence of problems. I have to get a grip. I'm going to write to her. Today, for example, I could let Rim know that I'm waiting for her. To do that, all I'd need to do would be to send Anna a text. Short, to the point: *Please tell Rim that I'm making her harissa spaghetti.*

And then go out and buy some.

THE PEIRENE SUBSCRIPTION

Since 2011, Peirene Press has run a subscription service which has brought a world of translated literature to thousands of readers. We seek out great stories and original writing from across the globe, and work with the best translators to bring these books into English – before sending each one to our subscribers ahead of publication. All of our books are beautifully designed collectible paperback editions, printed in the UK using sustainable materials.

Join our reading community today and subscribe to receive three or six books a year, as well as invitations to events and launch parties and discounts on all our titles. We also offer a gift subscription, so you can share your literary discoveries with friends and family.

A one-year subscription costs £38 for three books, or £68 for six books. Postage costs apply.

www.peirenepress.com/subscribe

'The foreign literature specialist'

The Sunday Times

'A class act'

The Guardian